BREAK LOOSE

A Hellhounds MC romance

Stacey Broadbent

Published by Stacey Broadbent, Ashburton, NZ
Copyright 2022 © Stacey Broadbent

Proofreading by Spell Bound
Cover image from Deposit Photos
Cover Design by Stacey Broadbent

ISBN: 978-0-473-66000- 0 (paperback)
        978-0-473-66001-7 (Kindle)

BREAK LOOSE

A Hellhounds MC romance

Stacey Broadbent

Author's Note

The characters in this story are from New Zealand, therefore UK spelling and terms have been used. Please remember these are not errors, it's just the way we do things here.

***Please also note* this story contains scenes of a graphic nature and may contain triggers, involving domestic abuse and violence.**

PROLOGUE

HOLDEN

"You look beautiful, Cami." Leaning against the doorframe, I watch my sister primp herself in front of the mirror. I've never seen her dolled up like this before, and I have to admit, it's weird. Round home, she's always been a jeans and t-shirt kind of girl, but standing before me is a woman in a knee-length dress of emerald-green, her hair pinned up in some sort of twisted bun, applying make-up to her eyelids. Hell, she's even wearing heels.

Her reflection glances at me with a grin, then she pokes her tongue out, and just like that, she's back to being my nineteen-year-old baby sister, Camira.

"Can you even walk in those things?" I nod towards the shiny black heels on her feet. "I don't think I've seen you in anything higher than a pair of Docs."

Cami snorts, twirling on the spot and making her dress dance about her legs. She takes two wobbly steps forward then stops, closing her eyes and taking a breath before taking another slow step forward. Holding her arms out wide, she grins. "Easy peasy."

I snort out a laugh. "Yeah, it looks it."

She folds her arms, a frown marring her face as she takes in my attire. "Please tell me you're not going dressed like that."

Reaching a hand up to the back of my neck, I avoid her eyes. "I'm not going."

"Excuse me? I don't think I heard you right, because for a minute there, it sounded like you said you weren't coming to my best friend's wedding." Her dark eyes blaze as her hands fall to her hips.

"Come on, Cami, don't be like that." I step forward, a hand reaching towards her, but she waves it away.

"How can you not go? She's like family. It's always been the three of us."

That's not entirely true. If it were, she wouldn't be getting married today. I bite back the words though, choosing instead to play at nonchalance. "I want to beat the traffic."

"You are *not* blowing off Darcy because of traffic. That's a cop out and you know it." Her eyes narrow, and I brace myself for what's coming next. "What's really going on? Are you in trouble?"

"No, it's nothing like that." *But I will be if I have to stand there and watch Darcy marry that jackarse.*

She throws her hands up in the air. "I can't believe you. First you decide you have to leave town, and on her wedding day, no less. And *now* you're not even going to bother being there for her." She shakes her head, her voice softening. "This is important to Darcy."

"I know it is," I say quietly, feeling like the biggest arse in the world. The day her father had a fatal heart attack, I'd sworn to always be there for her, but watching her marry Clay Ferriman is something I just can't do. The moment I laid eyes on him, I knew he was wrong for her. Riding with the Hellhounds, you get a feeling for people. You learn to spot the arseholes a mile away, and Clay… he's the biggest of them all. Just so happens, I'm the only one who can see it. The charm, the sweet-talking, the endless promises that never pan out. I know his type.

"You can't even spare ten minutes to watch the ceremony?"

I'd rather walk barefoot across hot coals than watch her make the biggest mistake of her life, but it's Darcy. And I'd do anything for her. Even if it tears my heart out.

"Okay, yeah. I guess I could swing by for a few minutes."

Cami's face lights up, then she punches me in the shoulder. "That's for making me get all hot and bothered." She turns back to the mirror. "Now I have to fix my face."

I park my bike across the street from the little chapel. Rows of seats covered in frilly bows face the floral arch by the steps, and beneath it stands Clay with his hands clasped in front of him. At least he made the effort to put a suit on and have a shave.

A lone guy breaks away from the milling crowd and heads in my direction. It takes a minute for me to recognise Matiu out of his leathers and in a pair of black slacks and a button-down shirt.

"Jesus, look at you," I say with a grin.

He slaps my hand, gripping my fingers with his before pulling away. "I know, right?" He tugs at the collar of his shirt. "I feel like a bloody idiot, but Cami made me promise to wear a shirt." He leans forward. "Your sister can be scary, man."

I bark out a laugh. "Don't I know it."

Matiu shoves his hands in his pockets, nodding towards the people all moving towards the seats. "You're not coming over?"

I shake my head, biting the inside of my cheek. "Nah, bro. I can't." I meet his gaze, and he nods.

"Fair enough."

"I just want to get one last look at her before I go."

"Sure that's a good idea?" His brows rise.

"No. I'm not… but I promised Cami too." I grin, but my heart's not in it.

"Maybe seeing it will make it easier."

"I doubt it. It hasn't made it any easier watching her walk around town with him." I grip the back of my neck. "I missed my chance. I waited too long."

Matiu slaps a hand on my shoulder, giving it a squeeze. "I'm sorry, man."

"Yeah, me too."

A forest-green Camaro with ribbons on the bonnet pulls up alongside the curb.

"That's my cue to leave." Matiu hooks his thumb over his shoulder. "Ride safe, brother. Don't stay away too long." He gives my shoulder one last squeeze then turns and jogs back to join the congregation.

The back door of the car opens, and Cami steps out. She catches my eye, giving a grateful nod in my direction before helping Darcy step from the back seat.

I catch my breath as I get my first glimpse of her. Long red hair cascading down her bare back with a simple veil clipped to the top of her head. The white fabric of her gown hugs every curve of her body, accentuating the roundness of her belly, and my stomach lurches as the reality sinks in. She's actually doing it. She's marrying him.

Her hair seems to float in the air as she glances over her shoulder, the sun glinting off her glasses. Her ruby-red painted lips stretch into a wide grin as I raise my hand in a wave. She lifts her own hand, her fingers wiggling.

Cami says something to her, and she pulls her attention back to the front, away from me. Soft music plays over the speakers, and Cami starts walking down the aisle, her hands clasping a bunch of tulips. Darcy's favourite.

Everyone stands, and the music changes as Darcy makes her way to the man she's marrying. The man I wish was me.

Dragging my eyes away, I push the ignition and rev the engine. I lower my helmet over my head and pull my shades from my pocket. With a kick of the stand, I pull onto the road, heading for the turn out of town.

I tried, Darcy, but it's too hard. I can't do this anymore.

CHAPTER ONE

HOLDEN

"Hey, Zeb, make yourself useful and hand me that 16mm spanner, would you?" I stick my hand out behind me.

"Geez, what'd your last slave die of?" Cami rests her hip against the bonnet, folding her arms across her chest.

"Here you go." Zeb passes me the spanner, his cheeks flushing red as my sister smiles at him.

"Don't even think about it."

His hands fly up. "What?"

"You heard me. Not a chance in hell, bro. Don't even try."

Zeb glances between my sister and me. "I wasn't—"

"But you were thinking it." I point the spanner at him with a pointed look. "That's my kid sister, and believe me, you couldn't handle her."

"Hey!" Cami slaps a hand across my back playfully. "He's right though." She looks Zeb up and down. "I'd eat you alive."

A wide grin spreads across Zeb's face as he turns on his heel and continues with detailing Aldrin's ember red 1963 Chevy Corvette. I don't know where the guy finds such great deals on these classics, but every time he brings one into us, it makes me consider joining the damn classic car club just to get my hands on those beauties. Aldrin certainly has an eye for them.

"Why would you do that? You've only gone and issued the kid a challenge." I shake my head. "I have enough on my plate without having to keep an eye on you."

Cami quirks a brow. "I've handled myself just fine while you've been away, brother. I don't need you to be my minder. I'm a big girl."

"That why you're here in the middle of the day instead of at work?"

"Can't a sister visit her brother without there being something wrong?" She pushes off the car and scans the toolbox before picking out a ratchet and handing it to me before I even need to ask.

She may not be able to figure out what she wants to do with her life, but the girl sure does know her way around an engine. I suppose that was bound to be the case hanging out with me and Matiu whenever we were tinkering in the garage. We always had some project on the go; converting a V6 to a V8, rebuilding Dad's Holden Camira engine from scratch, fixing up an old jalopy we found in the Buy Sell.

We were destined to be grease monkeys from the get-go, but I always thought Cami would do something big with her life. She's got an attitude on her that will serve her well in the field of her choosing. She just has to make the damn choice. Hell, I'm sure she could do an apprenticeship here if she wanted to. With her skills, Jericho would be crazy not to give her a shot.

"You and I both know you only visit when something's wrong. So spill." I straighten, wiping my hands down the front of my overalls.

"Ugh. I'm not liking this role reversal thing we've got going on." She flicks her finger between us. "I'm meant to be the one bailing you out, not the other way around."

"Jesus, Cami, what'd you do that needs me to bail you out?"

Her eyes flash as she places her hands on her hips. "Excuse me? You better not be giving me attitude when you know damn well how many times I helped you out back in the day."

She's not wrong. No matter what mess I got myself into, Cami was always there to back me up. Always.

I hold my hands up placatingly. "Okay, I'm sorry. What do you need?"

"Could I crash with you for a few nights?"

My eyes narrow. "Why? What's wrong with your place?"

She trails her hand along the bonnet, avoiding my eyes. "I just need a change of scene."

I don't buy it. "Cami?"

"What?" She juts her chin in defiance, her eyes darkening.

My jaw clenches. "What'd he do?"

"I think you mean *who*."

That son of a bitch. I'll fucking kill him.

"Don't get all Macho Man Randy Savage on me, bro. I already dealt with Derek and Miss Thang." Her lip curls at the very mention of them. "I just need somewhere to stay so I don't burn the fucking place to the ground with him in it. It'll only be a few days. A week tops."

"Jesus, Cami, you don't even have to ask. My place is your place, you know that." I pull her into my chest, wrapping my arms around her, and despite her bravado, she sags against me. "Sure you don't want me to sort him out for you?"

"And have you break the no-violence policy of your boys' club?" She snorts then hiccups as her shoulders begin to shake with sobs.

I crush her to me, resting my chin on top of her head. "Jericho would understand. Family comes first."

"Maybe a little roughing up would be nice."

"Consider it done."

"And… if anyone asks… I was with you all day." She raises her chin, peeking up at me.

"Okay?" I draw the word out, not liking what she's implying.

"I may have accidentally on purpose damaged some property on my way out the door." She bites her lip, her eyes darting behind me to the Ford Mustang I've been working on.

"You didn't…"

"I might've."

"How bad?"

She shrugs. "My keys might've been in my hand as I walked past."

"*Keys?* As in, more than one?"

She nods.

It's a dick move, but I can't say I blame her. That Torana is Derek's pride and joy. He is forever out there cleaning it and bringing it in for a tune up. He must've spent a fortune kitting it out with spoilers and rims, and in the blink of an eye, Cami has rendered it worthless. For the time being anyway. And Lawson's Lugs being the only garage in town that offers body work, he isn't likely to get it fixed any time soon either.

"Soooo?"

I let out a breath, laughing as I swing my arm around her shoulder. "Yeah, you were with me all day."

CHAPTER TWO

DARCY

Inspecting the glass in my hand, I determine it's up to standard before placing it carefully on the bench beside me. My hands fish about in the too-hot water, gathering the remaining pieces of cutlery and washing them quickly and proficiently. Somehow, I manage to do so without scalding myself, even though they feel as if they've been dunked in lava for the past fifteen minutes while I cleaned every other dish in our house.

I pull the plug and watch the water and bubbles swirl into a mini tornado before being sucked down the drain. My thoughts seem to follow, whisked away to a place I cannot reach. Grabbing the dish brush, I run it around the sink, letting the water run to wash away every last bubble. Once that's done, I wipe a tea towel around to dry it before adding it to the washing basket for tomorrow's chores.

With a fresh tea towel from the drawer, I dry each glass and dish, placing them away in the cupboards, along with the pots and pans, the cutlery, and the chopping board I used while making Clay's lunch.

The alarm on my phone rings, letting me know I only have five minutes before I have to pick up the children, and I silently curse myself for starting the dishes so late. I never should have let that nice man in a suit talk so long. I'd felt bad for him though, riding a bike around in the heat of the day. It was only polite to offer him a drink and hear what he had to say about his lord and saviour; even if I don't believe in that sort of thing.

Of course, Clay never would've let him get a word out. He'd more than likely have sent him packing with a few harsh words slung at his back for good measure. He doesn't take too kindly to strangers appearing out of nowhere, especially if they're men.

Still, it was nice to have someone different to talk to for a while. We don't get a lot of visitors out here, and it can get lonely when it's just me at home most of the day. Clay told me right from our first date I'd never have to work a day in my life if we were to wed, and he was true to his word. I've never had a job outside of being a mum and homemaker. Most important jobs there are, people say. Though it would be nice to be able to compare it to something else, see what I'm missing out on.

My phone rings again, and I toss the tea towel over the rest of the dishes. They'll have to wait. I can't be late for the children.

Locking the door behind me, I race out to the car and pull down the drive, a cloud of dust left in my wake. I'll have to check I didn't rough the dirt up too much when I get back home.

Traffic is busy, as it always is come three o'clock on weekdays, and I can already make out uniformed students walking in clusters down the road ahead.

I find a spot down the road a little from the preschool and have to power walk there. Molly's strawberry blonde curls bob as she runs to meet me with her satchel in her hand. Her big brother, Bobby, runs to catch up to her.

"Mummy, you're here!" Molly squeals as she flings herself into my arms. "I thought you forgotted us."

I nuzzle my nose against the softness of her cheeks, ignoring the way her warmth fogs my glasses. "I could never forget you, Molly doll."

"You're late." Bobby scowls, folding his chubby arms across his chest. "We're the last ones here."

I flick Miss Talbot an apologetic glance. "Sorry I'm late. I was away with the fairies, doing the dishes. Time got away on me. You know how it is."

Molly's eyes widen. "You were with fairies?!" Then her brow creases as she places her fisted hand against her hip. "I want to meet the fairies too. Why didn't you wait for me?"

I can't help but laugh. "Oh, I wasn't really away with the fairies, my love. It's a turn of phrase. It means

I was daydreaming." I trail my fingers across her frown.

She purses her lips for a beat, then smiles, wriggling out of my arms. "Okay."

I crouch beside my sullen-faced son and ruffle his hair. "How was your day today, Bobby? Did you have fun?"

He shrugs, but I can tell he's bursting to tell me something.

"You didn't have any fun? Oh, that just won't do. Maybe I need to tickle some fun into you?" I raise my hands, slowly moving towards his middle, but he quickly clutches his hands around himself, jumping backwards with a giggle. Like me, he's never liked being tickled, but he enjoys the threat of it immensely.

"No, Mum! I *did* have fun today, I promise."

I pause my fingers, quirking a brow. "Really?"

"Truly." He holds up his pinkie, and I wrap my own around it. "Pinkie swear."

"Well, alright then."

"Me and Troy built a big castle, like taller than you, eh, Miss Talbot? It was taller than Mum, wasn't it?"

Miss Talbot grins, playing along. "Oh yes. It was the biggest castle I think I've ever seen in my life."

Bobby beams up at me with pride. "See?"

"That's wonderful, darling. I wish I could've seen it."

"Bobby let me play in it too," Molly adds. "I was the princess of the castle, and Bobby was the king."

"That was nice of you to let your sister join in, Bobby."

He sniffs, shrugging his shoulders. "Troy said we needed a princess."

"And he's right. You can't have a castle without a princess, or a king." I take hold of both their bags, hoisting them onto my shoulder. "Anyway, I'm sure Miss Talbot would like to pack up now, so let's get going." I take their hands in mine, relishing the feel of their pudgy fingers.

The street is almost deserted by the time we make it out to the car, only a few children from the school next door still hanging around, waiting for parents. Molly and Bobby clamber into the car, and I toss their bags onto the front seat. We make it home in next to no time now that the roads have cleared.

The children take their bags and wait by the door while I inspect the drive and run the broom across to smooth out the patch I'd inadvertently kicked up in my haste.

When I'm satisfied it's back to the way it should be, I let the children inside and they race up to their rooms to put their bags away. I get stuck back into the dishes, eager to get them finished before making a start on dinner. Clay hates when dinner is late.

Molly and Bobby race back down to the kitchen, wrenching open the pantry door.

"Hey now. Is that how we do things here?" I ask, my hands on my hips.

"No, Mum." Bobby toes the pantry door. "Sorry."

I instantly regret my tone of voice. "It's okay. Here. Let me get you a snack." I usher them to the table and turn back to the pantry. "How about a freshly baked cupcake?"

There's an audible gasp before they both cry out, "yes!" in unison.

Chuckling to myself, I grab two cupcakes with fluffy blue icing from the container and put them on plates. I pour them each a glass of milk and set it down beside them.

"There you go."

"Wow, thanks, Mummy!" Molly plunges her tongue straight into the icing, licking a large blob off the top. "Mmmm."

While they eat, I get started on dinner. The steak has been marinating all day, just the way Clay likes it. I pull it from the fridge to come up to room temperature while I peel the potatoes and put them in a saucepan of water. I eye the clock on the wall, counting back to work out when to start everything. Clay will be home at five, and he likes his dinner ready and waiting on the table for him the moment he steps foot through the door.

As I wipe the benches down once more, there's a crash behind me and the unmistakable sound of glass breaking. My blood seems to freeze in my veins as I slowly turn towards the table.

Molly is staring wide-eyed at the broken glass lying in a puddle of milk in front of her. Her bottom lip trembles as Bobby jumps up, grabbing a wad of napkins and mopping up the spilled milk.

"It's okay, Molly-moo," he says, but there's no mistaking the tremor in his voice. He's scared. "Dad doesn't need to know, right, Mum?"

Snapping out of my stupor, I nod. "Right, baby. This will be our little secret." I rush to the table and pick up each shard of glass, resting them in the palm of my hand. I take the sopping napkin from Bobby and add it to the pile. "Why don't you take your sister into the lounge to watch TV?" I suggest, and his shoulders sag with relief.

He takes hold of Molly's hand and leads her away, her tiny shoulders heaving with pent-up sobs.

Emptying the detritus into the bin, I scan the area for any glass I may have missed and spy some glistening on the floor. On hands and knees, I brush the area around the table, careful to get every last piece, then do a quick sweep of the table too. I follow it up with some multi-purpose cleaner and a cloth, making it shine.

Next, I secure the rubbish bag and, even though it's only half full, I take it out to the large bin on the kerb. If luck is on my side, it will be collected before Clay notices anything is out of place.

I'm fooling myself, I know, but I have to believe it will work. I have to believe that for once, he won't inspect every inch of the house to find fault. That this time I'll get away with it.

CHAPTER THREE

HOLDEN

Jericho drops into the seat at the head of the table, steepling his hands in front of him. To his left is Stubbs, and on his right, Matiu. He clears his throat. "As you know, Hannibal Marx has taken over the Costello business. He's been busy cleaning house since Dante's death, but it appears he has resurfaced."

The last time Hannibal was around these parts, he'd aided his boss in kidnapping and torturing Jericho's old lady, Sam. We lost a good man in that fight and had several injuries. Hannibal's return can only mean more bloodshed.

"He wants to do business with us."

"Shiiiiiit." Matiu holds up his hand, still scarred from the bullet that had blown straight through care of Dante's goons. "Please tell me we're not going to."

Jericho spreads his hands wide. "Believe me, I want nothing to do with the prick, but I feel I owe him a meeting at least."

Stubbs snorts, folding his arms across his chest. "You don't owe him shit, Jeri."

"He had the chance to end Sam, *and* me, but he didn't. He called for help instead." Jericho gives us all a pointed stare, as if daring us to object. "It's just a meeting."

"About what?" I ask. "I thought we didn't get into his kind of shit, boss man."

"I don't know exactly, he just said he had a proposition to make and that it was all above board." He leans back in his seat. "No harm in meeting with the guy and hearing him out."

"Then I'm gonna be right there with you," Stubbs says, looking Jericho square in the eye. "I already lost one leader to that pack of mongrels, I'm not about to lose another."

Jericho dips his head in acknowledgement.

"When's this going down?" Matiu asks.

"Monday night. Hannibal's coming to meet with me here."

"Jesus, the guy's got some balls on him." I whistle low, lounging back in my seat. "Don't think I'd wanna show my face if I was him." I raise my chin at Jericho. "What's Sam doing while this is on? She need some company?" I give him a grin, running my tongue along my teeth.

He growls, his eyes narrowing. It's too fucking easy to rile him up.

He points his finger at me. "Don't think I won't beat your arse."

I chuckle, holding my hands up placatingly. "Now, now, no need for violence. We're a peaceful people, remember?" I grin.

Jericho shakes his head, but I can tell he's trying not to crack a smile. "Who the fuck let this guy back in?"

"You know you missed me."

"Next time I'll have better aim."

"So that's a no to babysitting Sam then?" I duck as a wad of paper comes flying towards my head and bounces off my shoulder.

Matiu coughs behind his hand. "Aim still needs work, old man."

"Don't you have a car to tend to?" Jericho stands, his signal the meeting is over. After Tony died, he couldn't bring himself to use the gavel, and it's now sitting in a glass case alongside a photo of our once faithful leader.

"Nah, I fobbed it off to Golden Boy over there." Matiu hooks his thumb in my direction, and I give his shoulder a backhand.

"You know, you could be good at your job too if you bothered to pay attention," I quip, shaking my head. "Someone spent all their time fiddling with rotaries, and it shows."

"Man, ain't nobody got time for no stinking rotary. Wash your damn mouth out." Matiu flings his arm around my neck, dragging my head into his chest. I wrap my arms around his waist, my leg snaking around his, ready to drop him.

"Jesus Christ, you two. Get back to work," Jericho growls as he shoulders past. "You got Aldrin's car detailed, Zeb?"

"All done, boss."

"Good. Hang with Holden and see if you can learn something while he finishes up." He turns to me. "Show him what you know."

"That won't be much." Matiu snorts, and I give him a gentle tap with my fist to his gut. "Oof."

"He'll learn a damn sight more from me than you, bro." I straighten, tapping the side of my head. "Every engine ever made is stored in here. There's not a thing I don't know how to fix when it comes to cars."

"Spoken like an overconfident jackarse." Matiu snorts, sauntering out the door and back through to the garage with his middle finger in the air.

"It's not overconfidence if it's true!" I call after him. "He's just jealous because I've still got pretty hands." I wiggle my fingers.

Zeb gives me a strange look, like he can't quite figure me out. I don't wait for him to make his mind up.

"Come on. Let's get this shit finished."

CHAPTER FOUR

DARCY

"That was delicious, wasn't it, kids?" Clay leans back in his seat, patting his belly.

"Yes, Daddy," Molly says with a grin. "I ated it all up, see?" She holds her plate up for him, and he smiles, rubbing the top of her head.

"What do we say, kids?"

They both look at me as I clear our plates. "Thank you, Mummy."

"You're welcome, my darlings."

Clay's thick arm weaves around my waist. "I think it's going to be this week. I can feel it."

"The promotion?" He nods. "That's great, Clay. I'm so proud of you." He's been vying for a promotion for years, but for whatever reason, they always seem to overlook him.

He pulls me onto his lap, and I quickly crush the plates into my chest to stop them from falling.

"Now look at what you've done," he mutters as he takes in my messy front. "What a pig. Right, kids?" He turns to them, scrunching his nose and snorting. "Mummy is a little pig."

Molly giggles, trying to snort too, while Bobby watches me with trepidation. I can tell he doesn't want to agree with his father, but he also doesn't want to get into trouble either.

I put on a smile, wiping my hand down my front and gathering the scraps onto the plates. "Silly Mummy, eh?"

"Go clean yourself up." Clay pushes me up from his lap, slapping me firmly on the bottom then laughing.

I carry the plates to the sink, rinsing them off and placing them on the bench. With a dishcloth, I dab at the smear of food on my shirt until there's just a large wet circle. I turn to see Clay staring at me, something shining in his hand. Bobby and Molly both sit, wide-eyed, beside him, their tiny faces pale.

"What's this?" His beady eyes narrow on me. It's a thin shard of glass. I silently curse myself for missing it. I'd checked twice, but I should've checked again. *Always check again.*

Without missing a beat, I take it from between his fingers and inspect it with pursed lips. "Just a bit of plastic I think." I step on the lever of the bin, but Clay places his hand on my shoulder, stopping me. His grip is firm, his thumb digging into my clavicle.

"I don't think so." He presses the tip of his finger to the point at the top and a bead of blood forms. He shoves it in my face, and I flinch back.

"P-plastic can be sharp sometimes," I stammer, taking a step back. His thumb presses deeper into my collar bone.

"Mummy?" Molly whimpers from her seat at the table, and Bobby shushes her.

"It's okay, baby," I croon, my eyes never leaving Clay's. "Daddy is just giving Mummy a cuddle."

Bobby takes his sister's hand and leads her down the hall away from the kitchen. I am both grateful to him for doing so and saddened that this is his life. That he knows to shield his baby sister from what's likely to happen.

Once they're out of earshot, I whisper, "It was an accident, Clay."

"Accidents only happen when people are careless. Were you being careless, Darcy?" He leans over me, his mouth twisted in a sadistic sneer.

"N-no, I—"

"So it was one of the children then." He straightens, turning his focus down the hall.

"No!" I grab at his shirt but quickly drop my hands as he turns his gaze on me. "It was my fault. I knocked over a glass when I was handing the children their snacks."

He tuts, shaking his head. "Always so careless with my things. When are you going to learn, Darcy?" He takes hold of my chin, squeezing it tight. "You think

I work my arse off every day so you can go breaking everything?"

"No, Clay. I don't. It was an accident. I swear, I didn't mean to do it."

"But you tried to hide the evidence, didn't you?" He stomps on the bin lever and peers inside. "Nothing broken in there."

"It's rubbish day tomorrow. I took the bins out." I glance out the window and he follows my gaze, seeing the bins parked at the end of the drive.

"Thought you could get away with it, huh?"

"No, I just…" I let my voice trail off as I try desperately to come up with a solution. "I uh… I was going to tell you. I have a replacement arranged already."

"And how much is that going to cost me?" It always comes down to this. *Money.* Ever since that first denied promotion, he's been overly focused on where every dollar of his pay cheque goes.

"Not a cent. The jar of chocolate spread is almost empty, and once I clean it out, it will make a fine glass. Just needs the label removed." I force a smile to my lips, hoping he'll accept it. "It looks just like the others."

"You want me to offer our guests a drink from an old spread jar?" His lip curls, as if what I'm suggesting is the height of indecency. Never mind the fact we never have guests around here, or the fact he wouldn't be the one serving them if we did.

"I'm sure I can make it look good as new with a soak in hot water."

"That right?" He sucks his teeth, raking his gaze down my body. "Maybe I should give you a good soak in hot water. Freshen you up a bit." He barks out a laugh, letting go of my chin with a flick of his hand. He swipes his beer from the table and takes a swig. "What're you standing there for? Hadn't you better clean this up?" He gestures at the table as he takes a seat, his legs spread wide. He watches as I clear the serving dishes and add them to the sink with the rest. He watches while I wring out a fresh dishcloth and wipe down the table and benches.

I fill the sink and wash the plates and cutlery, setting them on the dish rack to dry. When I'm done, Clay whistles from behind me. He holds up his empty bottle, and I take it from him, adding it to the recycling bin under the sink and handing him another. He makes a point of staring at the floor then towards the laundry.

"Shall I mop the floor?" I suggest, knowing full well that's what he's wanting. If I'd just done it in the first place, I wouldn't be in this position right now, being scrutinised.

"What do you think? We have children, Darcy." His tone is scathing as he shakes his head, as if I'm not the one who does everything for them. I bite back the desire to say something, knowing nothing good will come of it. The less I fight, the less the damage.

Instead, I nod, grabbing a bucket and filling it with soapy water. As I reach for the mop, I hear another whistle. Clay shakes his head, a sneer on his lips.

I close my eyes, my shoulders sagging in defeat as I grab a brush from the cupboard and get down on my hands and knees. It's going to be one of *those* nights.

Fighting back tears, I drag the wet brush across the floor, getting into every nook and cranny I can. I don't stop until the floor is gleaming and the bucket of water is a muddy brown. The whole time, Clay watches on from his perch above me.

CHAPTER FIVE

HOLDEN

Why I'm up at the ungodly hour of nine on a Saturday morning is beyond me. Though it could have something to do with the sound of my sister singing loudly while bending her body into all sorts of crazy positions. Cami warned me she was still an early riser and a yoga fanatic now, but I hadn't been expecting this. I always thought yoga was a silent exercise.

Still, now that I'm awake, my stomach is calling for coffee and something greasy, but my pantry is looking decidedly bare. I knew I should've stopped at the store last night before coming home, but it was

Friday and the boys were having a few quiets, so who am I to say no to that?

I pull up outside the supermarket, surprised to see it already bustling. Apparently, Brookhaven is a town of morning people.

Inside, I load a basket with the essentials; coffee, bacon, eggs, and beer. I toss in a bottle of wine for Cami too, hoping it'll stop her from waking me early tomorrow. As I scan the shelves for something to snack on later, a little girl with reddish blonde curls races past me, a dark-haired boy following with a scowl on his face.

"Molly, stop running!" a voice from my past calls from around the corner, and I instantly forget what I'm doing. I hadn't allowed myself to hope she'd still be here, and when Cami never mentioned her, I'd assumed she'd moved away. But I'd recognise that voice anywhere.

Down the aisle, the little girl skids to a halt, her brother nearly falling over top of her as he tries to stop himself in time. He takes her hand and drags her back my way.

"We have to stay with Mum, you know that," he grumbles as he stomps past.

Mum.

She has kids. Plural.

I mean, everyone knew that was why they were getting married; because he'd knocked her up, but I guess it never crossed my mind she'd go back for more. Then again, she was always so good with kids. I bet she's a great mum.

"Molly, you know better than to run off." She rounds the corner and crouches in front of the miniature version of herself. Her hair is longer and braided down her back, but it's still the same shade of reddish blonde it always was. Her oversized wire-rimmed glasses slip down her nose, and she uses her middle finger to push them back up.

When she stands, her eyes find mine, and there's a brief moment when I think she doesn't recognise me before she breaks out into a grin. "Holden?"

I hold my arms out to my sides. "In the flesh."

"I-I didn't know you were back."

"Been back about a month now. Haven't really been out much though. You know how it is." I grip the back of my neck, giving her a slow smile.

She drops one hip, twisting her foot against the floor like I remember her doing all the time. "How is Matiu?" She grins up at me, and my heart just about jumps out of my chest. She's stunning.

"Yeah, same old Matiu." I shrug. "Still giving me grief."

She eyes the patch on my jacket, her hand reaching for it then pulling away. Instead she nods towards it. "You're back in the club?"

"Never left, not really. The club is in my blood."

She nods again. "I remember."

"Mummy?" The little girl tugs on her sleeve. "Who is that man?"

Darcy's hand lands on the top of her head, smoothing her hair back. "This is Holden. He's an old friend of mine."

"Hi there." I wave, giving her a smile.

"I'm Molly." She bounces on her toes. "That's my brother Bobby."

The boy frowns at me. "Holden isn't a name, it's a car."

I chuckle. That's one thing I love about kids, they don't give a shit. They just tell it like it is. "You're not wrong. My dad is a bit of a car nut. He named me *and* my sister after cars."

"That's weird." He folds his arms across his chest, unimpressed.

"I suppose it is. But I'm a bit of a car nut too, so I don't mind it."

"Holden is a mechanic," Darcy offers. "And he rides a motorbike."

Bobby perks up at that. "You do?"

"I do. It's parked out front." I point through the window by the checkouts where my pride and joy shines in the early morning sun.

"Wow, cool." Bobby's feet seem to glide across the floor as he moves closer, his eyes glued to my bike.

Darcy laughs, the sound like a warm embrace. *God I've missed that.*

"I think you've made a friend for life now. He loves cars and bikes. Anything with an engine really."

"My kind of kid."

"He's pretty great. They both are." She smiles down at Molly, who takes advantage of her mother's attention and leaps up, latching her arms around her and attempting to shimmy up her body like a monkey. Darcy's cardigan tugs down her arm, exposing her shoulder and a dark bruise.

"What happened there?" I ask, and she quickly tugs her cardigan back up, wrapping it tightly around herself.

"Oh, nothing. It's nothing." She pushes her glasses up on her nose then ducks her head and takes Molly's hand. "We should get going."

I frown, not ready to let her go. "Darcy, wait."

"Holden, I can't. I have to go." She hurries down the aisle without another word, gathering Bobby on her way. They rush through the checkout and out the door without a second glance.

CHAPTER SIX

DARCY

Stupid, stupid, stupid. Why did I stop and talk to him? Not only did it dredge up old memories I'd tried to bury, but it's put me on his radar. He saw the bruise. It won't take him long to put two and two together because I wasn't smart enough to come up with a plausible excuse on the spot. I never was good at thinking on my feet like Cami was. Whenever we got ourselves into a pickle, it was always Cami who came up with some excuse that would let us off the hook.

God, I miss her.

I wonder what she's doing these days. Whatever it is, I bet she's kicking arse and taking names, as the saying goes. Of the two of us, she was the one with the most drive, the one destined for great things. She had a beautiful mind that could outsmart anyone, and even though she was a slight build, you always knew when she entered the room. Cami was a powerhouse, and I admired her. If I even had the slightest inkling of Cami's strength and tenacity, I would've left Clay years ago. Hell, I never would've gotten caught up with him in the first place.

I had been seventeen and shy, barely able to speak two words to anyone I wasn't familiar with. Clay had been twenty, working full time at Lyman's Seeds, and he'd found me fascinating back then. He'd spied me across the carpark outside the burger joint one night, and he'd pursued me relentlessly. Of course, being so young and inexperienced, I'd been extremely flattered by his persistence.

No man, besides my father, had doted on me like that. And with my father gone, I craved it desperately.

Cami thought he was a bit odd, and Holden outright hated him, but despite their warnings, I couldn't help the way my heart fluttered every time he said something nice. It made me feel seen, wanted. *Loved.*

Eventually, Cami came round, especially when I broke the news of my pregnancy and impending nuptials. Holden had distanced himself then, and I guess I understand why now. He could see something I couldn't.

And now I've gone and given him proof his feelings were justified. At least, that's how Holden will see it. If there's one thing I know about him, it's that he can't stand to see me, or Cami, hurt. He was protective of both of us, not that Cami ever needed it, but I'd appreciated it. As an only child, I'd always wanted an older brother, and by befriending Cami, I inherited Holden by default. Though, I have to admit, the thoughts I'd had about him were less than sisterly.

I didn't expect to see him back here if I'm honest. He left in such a rush, like he couldn't wait to be free of the place. I didn't even get to say a proper goodbye, just a brief wave over my shoulder before walking down the aisle. Had I known it would be the last time I'd lay eyes on him for five years, I would've taken my time, let my gaze linger on his a little longer.

Now he's back and I don't know how to feel about it.

I pull into the drive and cut the engine. The children clamber out of the car and race inside, while I sit a while longer, my head leant back against the seat. Holden hasn't changed one bit. He still has that boyish grin and dusting of stubble on his chin. And those blue eyes of his still make my heart race.

God, what am I doing? I'm a married woman.

A thump on the window draws my attention as Molly bounds by my door. "What are you doing, Mummy? Are you coming inside?"

Putting on a smile, I force all thoughts of Holden away and climb from the car. I give Molly the important job of carrying the toilet paper into the house while I grab the rest of the bags and trudge into the kitchen.

"You took your time," Clay says from his spot on the recliner. He hasn't moved a muscle since we left. "You buy the whole damn store?"

"No, it was just busy this morning." I load the bags onto the counter and start unpacking them.

"Mummy meeted a friend there," Molly offers as she drops the toilet paper on the floor. "He was really nice, and he had a motorbike, eh, Bobby?"

"Yeah! It was so cool, Dad. You should've seen it." He races around the house making an engine sound.

"Is that so?" Clay says through his teeth.

I can feel his eyes boring into my back. "Mmhmm. You remember Holden, right?" I turn to face him, trying to gauge his reaction. "Cami's brother?"

His eyes narrow, his foot tapping on the floor. "How could I forget?"

"He's, um, just got back into town."

"And you decided to meet with him in secret?"

Bobby stops running, and his head snaps round to me, worry creasing his brow. I give him a reassuring smile. He wasn't to know Clay wouldn't be happy about me running into an old friend.

"It wasn't a secret meeting, Clay. We just ran into him at the supermarket. I didn't even know he was in town until I saw him standing by the cereals." I grab the washing powder from one of the bags and walk on shaky legs through to the laundry.

"You expect me to believe you didn't know he was back?" The recliner groans with his weight as he pushes up to stand.

"How would I know, Clay?" I try to make light of it. "I haven't seen Cami in years." He made it pretty clear after our wedding that I was not to have friends over during the day while he was at work. Weekends followed, and before long, I had no one but Clay to rely on. Cami was my best friend, and I don't remember the last time we spoke. She's never met my children, and I have no idea what she's up to these days. She might have a brood of her own for all I know.

"Maybe you're meeting her in secret too." His breath is hot on my neck, and I have to force myself to hold still and not flinch at his sudden presence.

I turn, winding my arms around his neck. "I don't have time for clandestine meetings. I have too much to do around here." My fingers thread through the hair at the base of his neck, but he grabs hold of my hand, wrenching it down to his crotch.

"Damn right you do." He thrusts into my hand. I glance at the children in the lounge and back to him with a pleading look.

"Clay, please."

"This is your place. Right here."

"I know."

"You will not see him again."

"I wasn't—"

"Never. Again." He accentuates each word with a thrust. "You're mine. You belong to me."

I nod, blinking tears away. "I know," I whisper.

CHAPTER SEVEN

HOLDEN

Cami has finished twisting herself like a pretzel by the time I get home, and she's sitting at the bench with a coffee; something I'm sure negates all the hard work she just did. "It's just boiled if you want one." She tips her cup towards the jug. "I'd make you one, but I don't want to." She pokes her tongue out.

"There's that sisterly love I've been missing." I grab myself a mug and make a strong black coffee.

"Hey, if you wanted my love, you should've stuck around instead of going AWOL." She purses her lips, leaning back in her seat.

"Can we not?"

"Come on, man. You were gone for years. *Years*." She takes a sip of her coffee, then turns the mug around on the counter until the handle faces her. "You said you were only going for a few months. A year at the most."

I huff out a breath, raking my hand through my hair. "I needed more time than I thought. I'm sorry."

"Mmmhmm."

"Cami, I *am*."

"You never even visited." She pouts.

"I know. It's… complicated."

She rolls her eyes. "I'm sure it is." Sarcasm drips in her voice, and not for the first time, I wonder if she knows the real reason I left. I only ever told Matiu of my feelings for Darcy and why I had to leave, and even then, it was only because he guessed and tricked me into admitting it.

When I found out she was pregnant to Clay, I was devastated. But it was the engagement that did me in. She's the type of girl you marry and stay with forever. No turning back. I'd always seen her as my ride or die. I hadn't counted on anyone else stepping in before I had the chance.

Goddamn Clay Ferriman.

Clearing my throat, I try to act casual. "I, ah, ran into Darcy at the store." I take a sip of my coffee, watching surprise wash over my sister's face, followed by indifference. *Interesting.*

"Oh yeah?"

"Yeah. She seemed a little off. Ran out of there as fast as she could, like I'd scared her or something. Is everything okay with her?"

She shrugs. "As far as I know."

I shake my head. "She had this bruise on her shoulder. Looked pretty bad. As soon as I mentioned it, she bolted for the door."

Cami's jaw clenches, and she stares into her cup with a look that could turn water to stone.

"You never told me she had another kid."

Her eyes widen, and it's obvious she had no clue. *What happened while I was away?*

"Didn't I? Must've slipped my mind." She focuses her attention on her now empty coffee mug, spinning it around and around on the counter.

I reach out and stay her hand. "Cami."

She lets out a sigh, shrugging. "What?"

"What's going on? You two were inseparable. You have a fight or something?"

She scoffs. "Or something."

"What's that supposed to mean? When did you see her last?"

She holds my gaze, as if challenging me. "About two months after you left."

"Yeah, right."

She doesn't say anything, just continues staring at me.

"Shit. You're serious, aren't you?"

Cami leans back, opening her arms in a what-can-you-do motion.

"Jesus, Cami. That was almost five years ago. What the hell happened?"

"That jerk husband of hers happened. He started telling her who and when she could see people. Spoiler alert, it was no one and never."

Now it's starting to make sense; the bruise on her shoulder, the way she rushed away. I don't like it. Not one little bit.

"And you just let him tell you to stay away? That doesn't sound like you, sis."

"Oh, I put up a fight at first, but pretty soon it became clear Darcy wasn't interested in going against him." She laughs without humour. "I didn't even know she'd had the baby until I ran into her mum at the store."

What the hell? Darcy and Cami had been as close as two people could be from the age of ten. They'd done everything together and dragged me along for the ride too a lot of the time. Not that I was complaining. Even at twelve I could see something inside her. Something that made me want to be with her whenever I had the chance.

"I met them. The kids. A boy and a girl."

There's a flicker of something in her eyes. Jealousy perhaps?

"Yeah? Please tell me they don't look like their father."

I snort. "Thankfully, they take after Darcy. The girl is the spitting image of her. Only, she's got these curls." I wave my hand beside my head, a stupid grin on my face. "Cute as a button, like her mum."

Cami raises her brow, and it's only then I realise my mistake.

Clearing my throat, I continue, "And the boy is all serious. Protective of his sister. He liked my bike."

"Sounds like you had a good old catch up. I'm guessing the ball and chain wasn't with her then?"

"Nah." I shake my head. "Just her and the kids."

"Huh. Didn't think she was allowed out on her own." There's disdain in her tone as she goes back to spinning the cup on the counter.

"It's that bad? This thing with Clay."

"I don't know. She's still with him, right? So it can't be *all* bad. But I'll tell you something for nothing, there's no way I'd let a guy tell me who I can and can't see. That's some bullshit right there." Her voice is full of anger, but her eyes glisten with unshed tears of hurt and betrayal. "She's like his puppet or something."

"You ever think that maybe she doesn't *want* to be his puppet but has no choice?" A million thoughts run through my head, the most prominent that this would never have happened if I'd stuck around. If I'd been there for her like I promised.

Fuck. She needed us and we left her to fend for herself. *A puppet snagged on its own strings.*

"What are you saying?"

"I'm saying maybe she needed people to stick around and show her she wasn't alone."

"So it's my fault now?"

"No." I rake my hand through my hair, grasping the back of my neck. "But who else did she have? You and I abandoned her, and you know as well as I do that her mum was never the same after James died."

Her eyes flick side-to-side, a frown marring her face. "She still should've known she could come to me though." She glances up at me. "Right? It was always me and her. She should've known I'd do anything for her."

"I'm sure on some level she knows that, but if Clay was able to put a wedge between you two, then there's no telling what else he's done to make her stay." The very thought sends waves of anger through me. *What else has she been through?*

CHAPTER EIGHT

DARCY

Once bedtime stories are done and the kids are fast asleep, I head back down to the lounge where I know Clay is waiting. To his credit, he didn't lay a finger on me while the children were still up, but I know what's coming. I knew the moment Holden's name was uttered this morning.

Clay was protective of me from the very beginning, and he'd never taken a liking to Holden. He didn't like how close we were, and no matter how many times I assured him we were only friends, he wouldn't believe me. We'd had many fights behind closed doors about him, and even though I was heartbroken when he told me he was leaving town for a while, inside I'd been relieved. Without Holden around, it meant Clay wouldn't have anything to fret about and we could get back to being happy, like we had been at the start before jealousy raged its ugly head.

Only once the ring was on my finger, things took a different turn. We'd fought like all couples do, but after he lost the promotion, his whole demeanour changed towards me. He was quick to anger, possessive, and more often than not, he scared me. It only got worse once the children arrived; a new way to torment me.

The first time he hit me I was eight months pregnant. I was scared about the birth and desperately wanted my best friend by my side, but he refused, saying he was my best friend now. I'd argued that he was out working all the time, and I was lonely. Everyday tasks were getting harder to handle with my protruding baby bump and if he'd only let Cami come out to the house, I knew she'd give me a hand, make me feel less alone.

He called me ungrateful and slapped me across the face. It was so unexpected that I didn't even try to block it. My cheek had a raised red welt in the shape of his hand all that night. It hurt to touch. I spent the entire night trying to convince myself I needed to pack my bags and go, but by morning light, I'd not moved a muscle. Clay came out, dropped to his knees, and apologised. Promised it would never happen again. I believed him. Until the next time, when Bobby was merely six weeks old.

By then I was exhausted and emotional, and I thought he was justified in taking his frustrations out on me. I *wasn't* doing my chores around the house. Bobby was a needy baby who cried every time I put him down. It made it difficult to get anything done.

Now I accept my punishments for what they are; his need to control me, to wield power over me. I've learned how to take a hit with minimal damage to my insides. He avoids the face because I still have to pick the children up from care every other day, but anywhere that can be covered with clothes has bore the black and blue bruises of his fists or whatever is at hand at some point over the years.

When I step into the lounge and close the hall door behind me, he's waiting with his belt unbuckled and hanging from his fingers. An open bottle of beer sits on the table beside his recliner, along with a smouldering cigarette. I try not to wince at the thought of where that will end up.

"You make me do this, you know." He walks towards me slowly, dragging it out. From up close I can see his eyes are glazed. "I don't like having to punish you."

I know better than to argue. He likes me submissive and accepting of whatever he deems a worthy reprimand for my actions. Lowering my head to my chest, I stare at my feet, bracing myself.

"You got something to say to me?" His stale beer breath washes over me, and I swallow back the bile rising in my throat.

"Sorry, Clay," I whisper, knowing it's what he wants to hear.

"I didn't catch that." His hand flies out, grasping me by the chin and forcing my face up. "Say it again."

Staring directly into his eyes, I clear my throat. "Sorry."

"That's better. You know I'm only trying to protect you. Keep you safe. I can't do that when you go meeting up with people in secret. And in front of the children too." He shakes his head as if he's disappointed. "Not a good example you're setting for them now, is it?"

"No, Clay."

"We wouldn't want anything to happen to them because of your misdemeanours now, would we?" It's a threat he's made ever since Molly was born. I guess he could see how fierce my love for them was; yet another thing to cause him jealousy.

Jutting my chin against his grip, I clench my jaw. "No," I bite out.

His glassy eyes narrow, his hand tightening on my chin. "I don't like your tone." He raises the hand with the belt, letting it swing in front of my face.

I can't help flinching. I know the feel of the leather edges intimately, and as much as I want to stay strong, I can't. "Sorry," I whimper, fighting back tears.

He takes my glasses and folds them, setting them on the table, then turns me towards the recliner. He lifts my shirt over my head, the cool air pricking my skin. With his palm flat, he presses until I brace my hands on top of the recliner, curling my back.

"This hurts me just as much as it hurts you."

I doubt it.

"Mmhmm." I nod, gritting my teeth.

There's a whoosh, then a crack as the leather strap connects with my back. I want to scream but don't for fear of waking the children. Instead, I grip the chair and let silent tears fall to the floor. The second and third feel as though they split my skin wide open, and I'm sure I can feel blood trickle down my sides. By the fourth the pain is so intense I can barely breathe. My knees buckle beneath me, and I fall to the floor with a muffled sob.

Clay pants behind me, the belt slipping from his fingers. I pray to God it's over, but I know he still has one more tool on his belt. One more nightmarish way to teach me a lesson.

I curl into the foetal position, my arms wrapped around my legs and head tucked between my knees. My back feels as though it's on fire, but there's nothing I can do about it. Not yet anyway.

Clay crouches beside me, his sweaty fingers pushing hair from my face. He strokes down my arm, shifting it to rest on the floor in front of me. Once upon a time I would've given anything for him to touch me like this. To show me an inkling of kindness.

I smell it seconds before I feel it. The scorch of the cigarette as it's pressed to my rib cage, just below my armpit. He likes to mark me in places only he can see, like a badge of dishonour. I get one for using a tone with him, one for soliciting a secret meeting, and one more because he feels like it. Three raised burns in a line down my torso. If I had a marker to join them with the rest, I wonder what I'd see.

Clay comes back with a cool cloth and lotion. He dabs it gently on the welts on my back then drapes the cloth over them. It both stings and soothes, and a fresh batch of tears pool in my eyes.

"I only do this because I love you so much. You know that, right?" He continues bathing and dressing my wounds, taking care of me. It gives me whiplash how quickly he can go from anger to remorse.

He helps me up, guiding me down the hall to our room, where he eases me onto the mattress and under the covers, where I lie on my side. He tucks me in, careful to avoid my back. These moments after a beating are the only times he's tender with me anymore, and though it's ridiculous, a part of me laps it up. Like a love-starved child, I let him take care of me and whisper promises of love that I pretend to believe.

He perches on the edge of the bed, his head cradled in his hands. "It'll feel better in the morning," he says, but it's a lie. No amount of time can heal these wounds. "I *do* love you. More than I can bear sometimes, and it all gets on top of me." He thumps his chest. "It feels like my heart will explode with how much I love you, and when you do things like making secret arrangements, it scares me so much it hurts." He peers at me with tear-stained eyes. "I don't know what I'd do without you, Darcy. You're my everything. I couldn't bear it if you ever left."

It's the same spiel I've heard time and time again. A spiel that both soothes and confuses me. Sometimes I think it's almost worse than the beatings. At least with those I can see and feel the pain he's inflicted; unlike the drivel he shoves down my throat; calling it love and making me question myself.

Am I to blame?

Did I do the wrong thing?

Should I try harder?

Still, it's nice to hear the endearing words of love instead of insults and derision. I know it's crazy, sadistic even, but I've grown accustomed to it.

"You won't ever leave me, will you?" he asks in a voice so small you wouldn't believe it's the same man who only moments ago held a burning cigarette to my flesh.

I know what's expected of me. What I need to say to make him feel better about what he's done. And though it's the last thing I want to do, I say it anyway. "Of course not, my love. I'm yours."

He smiles then, and it almost reaches his eyes as he strokes his hand across my forehead, down my cheek, to the base of my throat. "That's my good girl."

CHAPTER NINE

HOLDEN

A black SUV with tinted windows pulls slowly into the yard. Everyone downs tools and makes their way out to the carpark. Though he says it's strictly business and above board, we want to show Hannibal just who's in charge around here. He's in Hellhounds territory now.

A tall, stocky guy with shaved hair and a scar along his cheek steps out from the front seat. He nods our way then opens the back door.

He's shorter than I expected, but he carries himself with an air of importance. His dark suit is tailored and looks expensive, but his boots are reinforced. An odd mix, but I get it.

You never can be too careful.

The door opens and Jericho strides out to meet him, flanked by Matiu and Stubbs. They stop a metre in front of him, Jericho folding his arms across his chest. "Hannibal Marx. Can't say I expected to see you again, but here we are."

Hannibal nods, the corners of his mouth twitching. "Presidency suits you, Jericho. Pity it was under such circumstances."

"It is what it is. We both lost people that day." The fact he used the word people and not men speaks volumes. He'd never lump Tony in with a scumbag like Dante.

"That we did."

"Shall we?" Jericho gestures towards the building, giving me a nod. Hannibal falls into step behind him. His goon stands guard by the car, his stance wide and arms clasped in front of him.

I round up the boys; work is over for the day. Cassian retrieves the sign from out front, and the roller door is lowered before we make a move towards the bar. Stopping in the doorway, I whistle at Hannibal's man. "You coming in or what?"

He tilts his head to each side before seeming to decide to follow us in. He parks himself at the bar, his body angled towards the back room where his boss talks with Jericho.

"You know what this is about?" I ask, nodding at Zeb, who takes up his position behind the bar. He opens a bottle of Jack and pours me a glass.

"Just the driver, mate." The guys sniffs, his eyes held firm on the door.

"Yeah, that's why you're built like a brick shit house and decked out like the secret service." The guy screams protection. What they think Hannibal needs protection from remains to be seen. He was the right-hand man to one of the closest things we have to gangsters here in New Zealand. If anyone knows how to look after himself, it's Hannibal Marx. The fact he brought Mr. Tough along with him makes me suspicious. Whatever they're discussing can't be as innocent as he made out.

I point to his ear, where there's a coil of wire attached to an earpiece. "What the hell is all that for?" I glance back to where we came in. "You got other men out there?"

The guy smirks but says nothing. I don't like it. We should've searched Hannibal before letting him in the room with our top dogs. Hell, we should've searched them both.

Before I can do anything about it, the door swings open and Sam strides through. "Who's is that SUV?" she demands, hooking a thumb over her shoulder. She stops short when she sees who is sitting at the bar, and her face pales. "Dustin?"

"Samantha." He nods in her direction then returns his focus on the back room.

Sam follows his gaze and her mouth drops open. "Is he…" She turns to me. "Who's in there with him?"

I hold my hands out placatingly. "Sam, calm down—"

"Don't tell me to calm down, Holden. Who. Is. It?" She speaks each word slowly and succinctly, as if spelling it out to a child. She has every right to be scared. The man behind the door did a number on her.

"Hannibal."

"What's he doing here?"

I shrug. "Wanted a meet with the boss man. All above board," I glance at the guy I now know to be Dustin.

"Dustin?" She folds her arms across her chest, waiting him out.

"Like I told him, I don't know anything about it." He pierces her with a stare. "I just drive."

"Nope." She shakes her head. "I know the Costello drivers. You're not one of them. Try again."

"Marx. The Marx drivers," Dustin corrects. "Hannibal got rid of them all when he took over. Wanted a fresh start. I guess I was the lucky one who got to stay." He smirks, placing his hands on his knees. The movement shifts his jacket, and I get a glimpse of metal at his waistband.

"Jesus, you packing?" I ask, jumping to my feet to stand between him and Sam.

Dustin grips the lapels of his jacket then slowly peels them open, revealing a side arm strapped to his waist. "I am, but I have no intention of using it unless necessary."

"And him?" I tilt my head towards the back room just as raised voices come from within, and before I can stop her, Sam races to the door, wrenching it open.

Jericho is in his usual spot at the head of the table, and beside him, Stubbs has hold of Hannibal, his arms pulled taught behind his back.

Dustin is up and pushing past, his gun drawn.

"Sam, get down!" I yell as I tackle the guy to the ground. His gun goes off, hitting the doorjamb above her head. Plaster and dust rain down over her as she ducks into the room, where Jericho pulls her behind him. He levels Hannibal with a stare.

"We agreed no weapons!" he barks, slamming his hands on the table. "I should've known better than to trust a Costello."

"It's Marx," Hannibal spits. "You put paid to the Costello name."

Jericho waves a hand dismissively, not bothering to correct him. Jericho had been tussling with Dante, but it had been Hannibal's own bullet that ended his life. "Same thing."

"It's not." Hannibal wrenches free of Stubbs' grip. "I'm not the same as him. I want to do things differently, but I didn't know if I could trust you." He turns to Dustin. "Stand down."

"But—"

"I said stand down." He adjusts his jacket. "It was just a misunderstanding, right fellas?"

Dustin lets the gun fall from his grip, and Zeb quickly darts in and kicks it out of reach. I keep him pinned to the ground all the same.

"Misunderstanding?" Jericho scoffs, his eyes narrowed on Hannibal. "Your boss knew better than to come around here expecting us to run drugs. That's not what we're about, and we never will be."

Hannibal raises his hands. "I know, but I had to be sure first." He reaches into his pocket, slowly. "Dante made a lot of enemies, you lot included. It ain't easy knowing who I can trust to bring into the fold, so to speak." He slides a piece of paper across the table.

"What's this?" Jericho asks, eyeing it with contempt.

"It's the real reason I'm here. It was never about drugs or solicitation. I had to test the waters first. You understand."

Jericho considers this a moment before nodding, taking hold of the paper. He signals to me, and I reluctantly let the big guy off the ground. I stick to his side, not willing to let him out of my sight.

Jericho scans the page briefly before glancing back at Hannibal with a raised brow. "You want protection?"

"In a manner of speaking. Like I said, Dante was not a loved man and by proxy, neither am I."

"So, we'd be like your babysitters or something?" Matiu pipes up, a grin forming on his face. "Shiiiit, Jeri, you ever think we'd be asked to look after the guy what kidnapped your Mrs?" He plucks a cigarette out and lights it up, taking a long drag. "That's some fucked up shit right there."

"Why us?" Jericho asks.

"Why not you? I've seen you in action, and I know what you're capable of."

"We had something worth fighting for." Jericho reaches a hand behind him, wrapping it around Sam's. "What makes you think we'd do the same for you?"

Hannibal shrugs. "I want the same things as you."

"I doubt it," I snort.

Ignoring me, he continues, "And you'll be well compensated, of course." Of course. The Costello name was synonymous with wealth, and as Dante's surviving 'heir', Hannibal would've inherited it all.

"We don't even live in the same town. My family built this place." He gestures to the surrounds. "Brookhaven is Hellhounds territory and we're not about to move because you ask us to," Jericho says.

"I wouldn't expect you to. In fact, I'm looking at relocating."

"Here?" Sam splutters, and Hannibal turns his attention to her for the first time.

"Yes." He takes a step forward, but Jericho blocks him. "I was following orders, Samantha. I had no choice."

She juts her chin up. "There's always a choice."

He shakes his head. "You know that's not true. I did what I had to, to survive. I never expected it to get so out of hand. We had a complicated relationship, you and I, but I thought we had an understanding."

Sam purses her lips. "I appreciated the kindness you showed me when you saw fit to, but regardless of that, you were still my tormentor."

Hannibal frowns, his shoulders sagging. "I know. I'm sorry. Believe it or not, you meant a lot to me. You were the closest thing I had to family, aside from Dante."

"Ah, this is all lovely, but can we get back to the part where you're bringing your business to Brookhaven?" Stubbs interjects, resting his fists on the table. "That's why we're here, right? To discuss business?"

"Hellhounds don't get involved in his type of business," I add. "At least we didn't last time I was here."

"Yeah, man, that's right, we don't." Matiu opens his mouth, popping his jaw and blowing a circle of smoke through the air. "You can't expect us to sit back and watch you run our town to the ground."

"That's not my intention."

"We're not seriously considering this, are we, Jeri?" I ask. "He's a drug runner, among other things."

"Not anymore. Yes, some of my dealings are, shall we say, less than legal, but I was never a fan of the drug running, *or* the trafficking."

"And we're just meant to take your word for it?" I scoff. "Not bloody likely, bro." I hook a thumb in his direction. "Can you believe this guy?"

"Okay, okay." Jericho holds his hands up. "I need to talk to my men about this."

"Of course." Hannibal straightens his jacket, moving towards the door. "I'll leave you to it." He tips his head to Sam then strides through the door, Dustin on his heels.

As soon as he's gone, Jericho pulls Sam into his arms. "Are you okay?"

"I'm fine." She pulls back, slapping a hand to his chest. "Why didn't you tell me you were meeting him?"

"Hoohoo, you're in trouble," Matiu sings, tossing his spent cigarette into an empty bottle.

Jericho casts a glare in his direction before taking Sam by the waist. "I didn't want to worry you unnecessarily. We had it covered."

"A little warning would've been nice. When I saw the car…" She pulls her lip between her teeth, and Jericho brushes his thumb across her cheek, leaning his forehead against hers.

"I won't ever let him hurt you again."

I toss my hand in the air. "I offered to keep you company, but Jeri was worried you'd fall for my charms and leave him. Ain't that right, boss man?"

Sam chuckles, wrapping her arms around Jericho's neck. "He knows he has nothing to worry about."

"Oh, sweetheart, that's only because you haven't seen me work my magic. Believe me, you'd be putty in my hands." I wiggle my fingers at her, and she buries her face in Jericho's chest, stifling her laughter. He growls, encircling her in his arms. Too easy.

Matiu laughs, slapping me on the shoulder. "Mate, I've yet to see this magic. When's the last time you got laid?"

Fucking traitor.

"I get laid plenty." *I don't.* And not for lack of trying. When I left, I made my way through woman after woman, but no one compared to Darcy. Not one. After a while, I gave up trying.

"It doesn't count if it's your hand, man," Matiu jokes, and I swat him away.

"At least I have full use of mine," I toss back at him with a smirk, and he sucks in a breath before pulling me into a headlock. I turn my head towards him, grinning as I slam my elbow into his ribs just enough to make him let go.

"Oh, it's on, bro." Matiu grins back, hunching his body into an attacking stance.

"Jesus Christ, you two. It's like wrangling children around here." Jericho steps in between, holding his hands out to each of us. "We've got other shit to discuss, or have you forgotten that already?"

I straighten, smirking at Matiu. My head snaps forward as Stubbs' hand connects with the base of my skull. Considering he's been around the block a time or two already, the old man can still move as silently and stealthily as the best of them. Matiu laughs his arse off, holding his hand up for a high five. Stubbs obliges.

"Missing half my fingers, but I can still smack you up the back of the head." He flips me the bird, though half of it isn't there, and he couldn't give two fucks either.

Rubbing the back of my head, I offer him my hand. "Touché, old man. Touché."

"Are we done?" Jericho demands, raking a hand through his hair. "I get why Tony was always in such a mood now. Jesus."

"You love us really, Jeri." I swing my arm around his shoulders, and he chuckles.

"I must be fucking insane, but I do."

CHAPTER TEN

DARCY

That car has been parked out front all morning. It's not one I recognise, and I don't know whether to bother Clay and call him or not. It could be nothing; a person parking up for a nap, someone taking a phone call, or perhaps checking a map. It is a particularly long stretch of road, and it wouldn't be the first time someone has come by asking for directions. Still, the fact it hasn't moved for several hours has me on edge.

On a whim, I grab a cardigan and wrap it around myself, covering the welts from my punishment—the belt somehow licked the tops of my shoulders as well as my back—and make my way down the long dirt drive.

As I draw closer, the figure inside begins to look familiar. The same chestnut hair only cropped in a stylish bob, the same perfectly straight nose, and when she turns to me with those same warm eyes, I almost collapse.

Camira.

My best friend all through high school. The one person I could tell anything… until I couldn't.

Her door opens slowly, and she steps out. "Hey, Darce, it's been a while." She props one arm along the door frame, the other held up in a wave.

"I…I…" I can't seem to form words. My hand flies to my face, pressing my glasses up farther on my nose.

She smiles at me. "You wanna go for a drive? Catch up?"

I can't help glancing behind me, even though I know he's not due home for another half hour. "I can't," I manage to say, pulling my cardigan tight. What I wouldn't give to get in beside her and just drive off and never come back. But I could never do that to the children.

She frowns, closing the door. "Okay, well maybe I could come in for a bit?"

Yes, yes, yes, I want to scream, but I know it's a terrible idea. If Clay comes home and finds her here, there's no telling what he'll do. I'm still days, maybe weeks, away from recovering from the last punishment he doled out. I don't think I could take another so soon after.

"I don't—"

"Come on, Darce. Just for a minute. I promise I won't stay long." She steps forward cautiously, holding her hand out as if I'm a timid animal in the wild. *God how I want to take her hand.*

I fumble with my cardigan, my feet shuffling against the dirt. "Maybe just a minute," I say, even though I know no good will come of it. I've never been able to say no to her.

"Great." She smiles, falling into step beside me. "I hear you have two kids now," she says, and the hurt in her tone shatters me. We had all these plans of her being the honorary aunt to my children, seeing as I have no sisters of my own.

I nod. "Yes, Bobby and Molly."

"Are they here? I'd love to meet them."

"No, they go to kindy on Tuesdays."

"Oh." Disappointment rings loud and clear, and another jolt of pain stabs my heart. "Maybe next time then."

I want to tell her that hers was the name I wanted to call when I felt the pang of my first contraction, not Clay's. That she was the one I wished was beside me, holding my hand and encouraging me while my body felt as if it was being torn in two. I want to tell her that I'd picked up the phone to call her so many times over the past few years, but I don't. What good would it do now?

Instead, I stay quiet, listening to the sound of dirt and stones crunching beneath our feet. When we get to the door, I ease it open, and a wave of nausea washes over me. If Clay knew she was here, he'd be so angry.

"I like what you've done with the place," Cami says, gesturing to the walls I'd spent hours painstakingly painting whenever the children were asleep. Growing up, our house had never had much colour, and I thought the bright airy feel the paint gave the rooms would somehow make the loneliness and pain seem less. It doesn't.

"Thanks." I stand by the door, my hands clenching and unclenching against my cardigan, one ear listening for the sound of Clay's car.

"Darce?" Cami calls from the living room, then her head pops around the corner. "Oh, ah, okay then." She leans against the doorframe opposite me. "I can tell I've caught you at a bad time, so I won't keep you. I just wanted to check that you're doing okay?" Her voice goes up at the end, as if asking me a question.

I force a smile to my lips. "I'm fine."

She frowns. "I don't think you are."

"I don't know what gave you that impression," I start, but she reaches out, her palm landing on my arm.

"Darce, it's me you're talking to. I know you like the back of my hand."

I pull back, wrapping my arms around my middle. "Did Holden say something?"

"He's worried about you. So am I."

An odd sounding laugh falls from my lips as I drag my glasses from my face and clean them against my top. "There's nothing to be worried about."

She gasps, her hand flying to her mouth. "Darce, did he do this to you?" She grabs hold of my arm before I can pull back. One side of my cardigan has slipped down, revealing not only the purple and blue bruise, but also the welts from the other night. Her eyes brim with tears.

"It's not what it looks like." I fumble with my glasses, dropping them then stooping to pick them up. "I'm just clumsy."

"That's not clumsy, that's assault."

I wrench the door open, standing aside. "You need to go. You don't know what you're talking about."

"I can help you. You don't have to put up with this."

I jut my chin, licking my lips and staring out the door. "I made my bed."

"Jesus, Darce, that doesn't mean you have to stay! You made a mistake, and that's okay. But you don't have to stick around."

"Of course I do," I seethe.

"Don't give me that bullshit. Think of your children."

My head rears back as if I've been slapped. "I *am* thinking of them. They're why I stay."

"So they can see their dad beat the shit out of their mum?"

"It's not like… He doesn't do it in front of them," I croak out, my voice thick with unshed tears.

Her eyes soften and she reaches for me again. "Just because they don't see it, doesn't mean they don't know."

I know that. Of course I do. But knowing it and seeing it are two different things. I make sure to keep them out of it.

"No kid should have to bear witness to that, Darce. Not even from behind closed doors. And…" She pauses, her lips pursed. "How long before he turns his hand to them?"

I shake my head fervently. "He wouldn't." But even as I say the words, I know they're not true. He's threatened me with that very thing multiple times. It's how he keeps me in line.

Cami shakes her head sadly. "If you believe that, you're crazy."

"I…" My bottom lip trembles, and I pull it between my teeth. I can't let this continue. Clay will be home any minute, and she can't be here. "You need to go."

She stares at me for a beat before nodding. "Okay, I'll go." She takes my hands in hers, forcing a crumpled piece of paper into mine. "But you call me if you need me. Any time, day or night." She leans in, kissing my cheek. "Promise me."

I frown, uncomprehending as to why she's doing this. We've had no contact over the years, and now here she is, offering me a lifeline.

"Darce, I'm not leaving until you promise me."

I hesitate, but only for a second. I need her gone before Clay gets home and sees her. Shoving the paper into my pocket, I nod. "Okay, I promise."

CHAPTER ELEVEN

HOLDEN

"You were right," Cami says as soon as I walk through the door.

"I'm sorry, could you repeat that for the fellas at the back?" I cup a hand to my ear, grinning at her.

"Pfft, you'll be lucky. I've said it once, and it pained me to do so. I'm not about to say it again." She tilts her glass at me with a raised brow. I nod, sliding onto the stool beside her.

"So what am I right about?"

Unscrewing the cap off the bottle of Jack, she pours a glug into another glass and pushes it across the counter. "You might want a drink for this."

"Oh Jesus, Cami, what've you done now? Please tell me you didn't go back and torch Derek's car."

She smirks, her eyes lit up. "No, but that's not a bad idea."

"Cami," I warn.

"Joking." She holds her hands up, then her brow furrows and she takes a sip of her drink. "Seriously though. I think you were right about Darcy needing our help."

She has my attention now, and she's right, I will need a drink for this. Tipping my glass back, I down it in one and reach for the bottle for another.

"I went by her place today. She was skittish as hell. Kept watching the door and telling me I needed to leave. She had these marks on her back." She hovers her hand above her shoulder. "I thought he was just controlling, you know? Like wouldn't let her see people. I never imagined he was hurting her like that." Tears pool in her eyes. "It's so much worse than I thought him capable of."

My jaw clenches as she confirms my suspicions. I knew something wasn't right.

"We have to do something, Holden. We can't leave her out there with him." She lifts her glass to her lips with a shaky hand.

"We can't just rock on up and kidnap her either." As much as I'd like to, there's still the possibility she won't want to leave. What do they call it? Stockholm Syndrome or some shit?

"How could I let this happen?" She grabs the bottle and tops her glass up, almost to the brim.

"Woah." I take the glass from her and place it on the bench. "I don't think the answer is to drown yourself in booze, sis. You can't beat yourself up over this."

"I can and I will. She was *my* best friend. I should've realised what was going on instead of sulking and turning my back on her." She wipes her nose with the back of her hand, sniffing.

"You weren't to know."

She shakes her head. "*You* knew. You never liked him. And I could never figure out why. But you knew, didn't you? You knew he was… wrong."

"And yet I did nothing about it."

"You're my big brother. It wasn't your place to, it was mine. I should never have let him cut me out of her life. I never should've left her alone with him."

"Look, Cami, it's done. It's in the past and we can't change that. What we *can* do, though, is help her now."

She nods, but I can tell she's going to continue blaming herself.

"I gave her my number and told her to call me anytime," she offers.

"Well, that's a start."

"Do you think we should call Topher? Get him to do some house calls?"

"Topher? What's he got to do with this?" The last I heard, Topher Grayson was bricklaying with his old man after my sister left him high and dry. They'd been together all of six months, and he took the break-up hard.

She snorts, sliding her glass back towards her and lowering her lips to the rim, slurping a mouthful. "I keep forgetting you haven't been around for a while. He's the sergeant in town now."

I quirk my brows. "Bronson?"

"Promoted to senior sergeant once Alf Gibson retired."

"Jesus. Things really *have* changed."

She huffs out a laugh. "Right? Surprised the shit out of me too, but here we are." She stares into her glass as if the answers to life's questions can be found at the bottom. "So, you think we should tell him?"

"I don't know. It could make things worse for her if the cops start sniffing around."

"Shit, you're right. I didn't think of that."

"Maybe we take turns swinging by during the day. He still works at Lyman's Seeds, I take it?"

"As far as I know. The way she was acting, I'd say he comes home for lunch most days."

"We can work around that." For once, my sister being jobless has its uses. "You swing by mornings, and I'll cruise by in the afternoons. If I'm not able, I'll get Matiu to. He won't take much convincing." Placing my hand on her shoulder, I give a reassuring squeeze. "Between the lot of us, we'll make her see sense. We'll get through to her."

"What if it doesn't work?" she asks, her voice soft and so unlike her usual loud and obnoxious tone.

"Then we do what we have to, to protect her."

She nods. "Okay. Whatever that means, I'm in."

"I think you know what it means." I flash her a pointed look. "Fuck-knuckles like Clay only understand one language, and it just so happens I'm pretty fluent in it." I flex my fists in front of me. "If it comes down to it, I'll deal with him, and you get her and the kids out."

Cami gives me the side-eye, swirling the remains of her glass. "She means… a lot to you, doesn't she?"

I snort. "What kind of question is that? Of course she does. She was practically part of the furniture throughout high school." I snatch the bottle up and refill my glass, avoiding her stare, but I feel it boring into the side of my skull.

"Mmhmm," is all she says.

"What?"

"You're willing to break the no-violence code for her?"

"Of course I am. Just like I would for you too. Clay needs to learn to pick on someone his own size instead of taking his frustrations out on those who can't, or won't, fight back."

"And if Jericho catches wind of it?"

"Jeri will understand. Darcy is family, and family always comes first.

CHAPTER TWELVE
DARCY

He's back again. Ever since Cami's impromptu visit last week, Holden has been circling the block each afternoon, and she parks up out front each morning after Clay leaves for work. They never come in or try to talk to me, just sit there, watching. I don't know what they're playing at, but it has to stop. Eventually, Clay is going to see them, and I'll be the one who gets the blame.

I pull the plug on the lunch dishes and dry my hands on a tea towel then slip on some shoes. My stomach is all in knots at the prospect of seeing him again, and even though I know it's wrong, I can't help but glance in the mirror on the way past to make sure I'm presentable.

As I make my way down the long drive, I watch him pull his bike around and park it up under the trees across the road. At least he has the sense to somewhat hide it in case Clay returns early.

Holden pulls his helmet from his head and swings his leg over the back of the bike, dismounting. He swaggers across the road, stopping at the end of the drive and leaning against the fence post.

My throat goes dry, while my palms turn clammy, and I have to wipe them against my jeans. He hasn't changed one bit from the boy I practically grew up with.

"Hey, Darcy." He grins at me, the corners of his eyes crinkling.

"Holden," I say breathily, then laugh and clear my throat. "What are you doing here?"

"Oh, you know. Getting some fresh air." He turns his gaze skyward, inhaling deeply. "There's something about the air out here, you know?"

I suck in a breath myself, nodding. He's right. It was one of the things I'd loved about this place when I moved in. Funny how you forget such simple pleasures over time.

"How've you been?" His eyes travel up and down my body as he asks, and I automatically wrap my arms around my waist.

"Good." I nod, offering what I hope looks like an honest smile. If I can just make him see that everything is fine, they'll stop this craziness and leave me and my marriage in peace.

Peace.

I snort inwardly. I haven't known the meaning of that word in a very long time. Perhaps stagnation would be a better word. No, that's not strong enough. Disarray? Disruption? Despair?

Yes. Despair is far more appropriate.

"You don't need to do… whatever it is you think you're doing," I say, scrunching my nose. "I'm fine."

Holden raises a brow, folding his arms across his chest. His biceps strain against his t-shirt, and though I try to stop them my eyes land on the muscles as they flex.

"I don't know what you're talking about."

This time it's me who quirks a brow. "This tag team thing you and Cami have going on."

He shakes his head, smirking. "Nope. Not following."

I frown in confusion. Could I have this all wrong? Is it possible he really was just coming out for some fresh air then saw me approaching?

Heat flames my cheeks, and I take a step back. *So stupid, Darcy. Of course Holden Hart's not here to see you.*

"Oh, okay." I glance over my shoulder, back toward the house. "I'll just…" I hook my thumb that way and turn on my heels before the tears that threaten fall.

"Darcy, wait." His fingers wrap around my wrist, stopping me in my tracks. I wheel around, staring at his hand until he let's go. "Shit, sorry." He rakes a hand through his hair. "Can we start again?"

"Start *what* again, Holden?"

"Goddamn it," he hisses under his breath. "I'm fucking this all up."

I don't know what he wants me to say, so I just stay silent, waiting him out.

"I didn't mean to make you feel… whatever that was." He waves his hand out. "I was just joking around, like old times. I guess we're not there yet."

Memories of him having me on when we were younger flash in my mind. He always liked to pretend he didn't understand what I was saying, and it would drive me insane. Sometimes I'd even chase after him in mock frustration, when inside I was giddy with the thought of catching him. Not that I knew what I'd do if that ever happened, but the idea was enough.

Back then, it'd been all in fun and I knew that, but now, I apparently can't tell the difference between friendly jest and scathing remarks that leave me filled with crippling doubt.

"Sorry," I mumble, ducking my head.

"Hey." He's right in front of me in a matter of seconds, his thumb and forefinger cradling my chin as he raises my gaze. It's so different to the way Clay wrenches my face up with his vice-like grip on my chin. "You don't have to apologise. It was my fault."

I stare into those all-too-familiar eyes and feel myself crumble. I don't remember the last time Clay looked at me with such reverence, such adoration. Perhaps he never did. Perhaps our romance had all been in my head. It certainly feels that way these days.

My voice catches in my throat, and when I open my mouth to speak, nothing comes out but a breathy exhale.

"You don't ever have to apologise to me." He presses his forehead to mine, and my eyes flutter closed. "Not ever."

A sob escapes my lips as I fall against him, and he wraps me in his arms. It feels so good to be held by someone other than my children. Someone who can hold *me* together, who can be strong for *me*.

"Shhhhh," he whispers against my hair. "You're okay. I've got you."

But I know it's a lie. The only one who's got me is Clay, and if he were to see me in Holden's arms, there's no telling what he'd do. So I do what needs to be done. I fight against every cell in my body and step out of his grasp, putting distance between us.

"I can't." I shake my head. "You need to stop coming."

"Darcy, no—"

"Holden, please." I force myself to meet his gaze. "It'll only make things worse."

"But—"

"Just go." I spin on my heels and hurry back up the drive before I can change my mind.

CHAPTER THIRTEEN

HOLDEN

"I can't believe we're doing this," Matiu complains as he stomps ahead of me. "Shot in the hand, and now I have to protect the dumb fuck who did it."

I snicker. "Wasn't it one of the others who shot you?"

He glares back at me. "Same thing, man."

"Whatever, bro. Jeri says we can trust him, I guess we gotta trust him." Of course, I'm talking out of my arse right now. I have not one iota of trust in these guys. I don't give a shit if Hannibal and Jericho have come to some sort of agreement; something just doesn't sit right with this.

"Pssh, you've changed your tune. I thought you didn't like them either."

"I don't. But I don't have to like them to do my job." I stop at the door and turn my back to it, folding my arms across my chest.

Matiu follows suit. "Yeah, well, if it comes down to it, I ain't taking another bullet, that's for damn sure. Not for these fucks anyway."

"You and me both, brother." I hold my fist out to him, and he bumps it with his own.

"What do you think they're doing in there anyway?" Matiu nods his head towards the door.

"Right now? Nothing. They're not here yet, numbnuts." I chuckle. "Fat lot of good we'd be as security if we showed up after the fact."

A few minutes roll by and then a black SUV rolls up to the curb. Dustin climbs out and opens the door for Hannibal. "Gentlemen." He nods, adjusting his jacket. He waits while Dustin opens the door and checks the room.

"No one's been in or out," I say.

"Can't be too careful."

With Dustin's all clear, Hannibal strides through the door, closing it behind him.

Matiu snorts. "He really thinks he's the shit, don't he?"

"You're not wrong there. What's the bet the Hellhounds are the only ones who actually have beef with him?" I chuckle, shaking my head. "Dude takes himself way too seriously."

Another SUV, this one a deep forest green, pulls up behind Hannibal's.

"The fuck is this guy?" Matiu says, shuffling his feet.

"The guy he's meeting, I guess." I watch as a Dustin-wannabe steps out of the driver's seat and walks around the front. He stops at the back passenger door and opens it, bowing. A short man with thick black hair and a round belly steps onto the curb.

"Mr. Takanawa to meet Mr. Marx," the driver says, waving his hand towards his companion. "They're expecting us."

I nod then hold up a hand to stop them. "One moment." I knock on the door and push it open like some sort of assistant. I sure as shit made some bad life choices to be acting like Hannibal's secretary. "Mr. Takanawa's here," I say through gritted teeth.

"Send him in."

Swinging the door open, I usher the man through and close the door behind him.

"Mr. Takanawa's here," Matiu mimics in a voice much too high to be accurate. "You missed your calling, man. Being Hannibal's bitch suits you."

I thump his arm with my fist, and he cracks up laughing.

"You're one to talk. Aren't you on the way to having a chain attached to your balls?"

His smile falters, and he shrugs his shoulders a couple times. "Barb's not like that, man. She's cool."

"Mmhmm. And Sam is too, but she still holds Jeri's balls in her purse."

Matiu snickers. "Don't let *him* hear you say that."

"Seriously though, how's it all going? Has she turned into a bridezilla yet?"

His eyes widen, and he leans in. "Mate, she lost the plot when she found out the dress she wanted couldn't be made in time." He leans back, shaking his head. "Scariest shit I've ever seen, and I've been threatened by your sister and shot in the goddamn hand." He holds his hand in the air, as if I haven't seen it a dozen times already.

"So, it's going well then?" I joke, chuckling. I honestly never thought I'd see the day Matiu settled down, but after meeting Barbs, I'm not surprised he put a ring on it. That girl loves him like nothing else. Hell, she walked into a goddamn battlefield with him, hand-in-hand, to save Sam. The chick's got some balls on her, and she's about to add Matiu's to the collection.

"I don't know what the big deal is. It's not like it's gonna stay on her for long anyway." He chuckles, pulling out a cigarette and lighting it. After a long drag, he says, "She'll be butt naked by the end of the night, may as well start off that way, eh?"

"Jesus, bro, I hope you didn't say that to her." I shake my head, laughing along with him. The dude has a serious death wish if he thinks any bride is going to show up in something other than a fucking wedding dress.

"Shiiiit, man, you think I wanna have my dick in a sling? I ain't that stupid."

I tilt my head to the side. "That's debateable."

His fist comes out of nowhere, thumping my arm. "Rather be a stupid prick with a woman than a smart cunt without." He grins, waggling his brows at me.

"Yeah, about that." I sniff, turning to face him. "I thought you were gonna keep an eye on her for me while I was away?"

"Who? Darcy?" He frowns. "I kinda thought that ship had sailed, mate. I mean, she married the guy."

My jaw tenses. "I remember. I was there."

"Woah." Matiu holds his hands up. "What the fuck's your problem? You're the one who left. Sorry if I thought you'd be over it by now."

I suck a slow breath in through my nose and close my eyes. I don't want to deck my best mate, but he's pushing it.

"I thought I would be too, okay? But you don't just *get over* someone like Darcy Fields." I refuse to call her by any other name.

"Jesus, okay, man. Chill." He offers me his cigarette, and even though I've never smoked a day in my life, I take it. The foul smoke scalds on its way down my throat, and I cough.

"Fuck, that burns. Why the fuck do you smoke this shit?" I ask as I hand it back, thumping on my chest.

He takes another puff before answering. "Because it relaxes me." He taps his temple. "Quiets all the shit in here."

I quirk a brow. "Bro, if this is your brain when it's quiet, I'd hate to know what it's like when it's not."

His eyes widen. "It ain't pretty, man, I'll tell you that for nothing." He holds what's left of it up in front of his face, as if he's trying to make sense of it himself. "What's the deal with Darcy anyway? Why you so bent outta shape about her?"

Where do I even begin? I've been in love with her for as long as I can remember? She married the wrong man?

She's hurting.

"I ran into her last week, and again a few days ago." I don't bother telling him just how I ran into her a second time. "She's… things aren't good, man."

He flicks the cigarette butt to the ground and stomps on it. "Like how?"

"Like I think he's beating her." Both my jaw and fists clench, as they always do whenever I think of her out there with him.

"Shit, man, for real?"

I nod. "Yeah. She had bruises on her, and she's nervous as fuck, withdrawn; more than she used to be."

"Motherfucker." He curls his hands into fists. "What are we gonna do about it?"

This is why he's my best friend. I don't even have to ask and he's ready to have my back. The thing is, I still don't know what to do, not when she runs every time I get near her.

"I'm still trying to work that out. At the moment, me and Cami are taking turns driving past her place until we figure out the rest."

"Well, whatever you need, I'm with you. No questions asked."

Chapter Fourteen

Darcy

"Good morning." Clay pads through to the kitchen, taking his seat at the table. I've already placed the newspaper there for him and his coffee; black with no sugar, just as he likes it.

"Morning, Daddy," Molly says around her mouthful of cereal, a dribble of milk hanging from her chin.

"Morning, Molly-moo." He ruffles her hair, and she beams up at him. It's not often he pays her attention before he's had his morning coffee, let alone uses the name he coined when she was only a baby.

"Do you have to go to work today?" she asks.

"Just like every other day of the week." He flicks the paper, scanning the headlines. "Why?"

"Silly Daddy." She giggles, glancing at me with an amused grin. "Today is the fair. Can you come?"

The paper falls from his hands to the table, and he turns his full attention to her. "What fair?"

"At preschool! Mummy will be there, won't you? She's baking cupcakes!" She licks her lips with all the excitement a three-year-old can muster.

"Is that so?" He casts his gaze to me, one eyebrow raised. I can't tell if this is one of those times he's going to turn it into a big deal and forbid me from going, or if he's genuinely interested.

"Uh, yeah. They asked for parents to bring along a plate of baked goods to sell. They're raising money for a new play gym." I plaster a smile on my face. "I thought I told you." I know for a fact that I did, but it's no surprise he doesn't remember. Unless it affects him directly, he tends to ignore most of what I say.

"You didn't." His tone is clipped, and my shoulders sag in anticipation of what I'm sure is coming next. Molly will be so disappointed if I can't come. And to be honest, so will I. The few times a year when I can get out and see other adults are, sadly, my highlights. I even sent a message to Cami to tell her about it on the off chance she can come. It's the perfect excuse for me to see her again, and for her to meet the kids. I know I'm tempting fate, but after talking with her last week, I haven't been able to stop thinking about her or Holden and how much I've missed them.

"It's just a fun day for the kids with games and prizes, and a bake sale."

"I'm going to win a prize." Molly puffs her chest out. "Bobby said so. He's in charge of the hopscotch, and he said I can win."

I can't help the smile that forms at her innocence. "I'm not sure that's how it works, muffin, but if you try really hard, I'm sure you can win something."

"No." She shakes her head indignantly. "Bobby said *everyone* wins." She folds her arms across her chest.

"Oh that's a lovely idea, isn't it?" I smile at Clay, hoping he'll not ruin this for her.

He snorts, picking the paper up again. "You can't all be winners."

Molly's face drops. "But Bobby said we could."

"I guess we'll just have to wait and see, won't we?" Darting around the counter, I take up her bowl. "Have you had enough?"

"Yes, Mummy."

"Right, why don't you go and finish getting dressed? And I'll make a start on these cupcakes." My eyes flick to Clay, but he makes no move to correct me.

Molly jumps down from the table and races down the hallway, singing at the top of her voice. If Bobby wasn't already awake, he will be now.

"Is this thing open to the public?" Clay's eyes remain on the paper in front of him, but I can hear it crinkling between his fingers as he clenches. This does not bode well.

I busy myself at the counter, rinsing dishes and wiping the bench. "Um, I think so, yeah. But it'll mainly be parents I'd say." Keeping my back turned to him, I rifle through recipe books until I find the one I want. Perhaps if I just carry on, he'll leave it be.

"And you'll be there all day?"

"I was planning on it… unless there's something else you need me to do?" I let my question hang in the air.

"What time does it finish?"

And there it is. His excuse to keep me from attending; who else is going to cook his dinner?

Flicking through the book, I find the page I need and place it on the recipe stand. "Same time as preschool closes. 3PM. I'll still have plenty of time to get dinner ready after we get home." It's then I turn to him with a smile before grabbing my apron from the hook on the wall. I glance at the clock. "I've even got time to make a double batch of cupcakes if you like. One to take and one to keep?" A little buttering up never hurts.

He purses his lips, then grabs his coffee, taking a large gulp. He leans back in his seat with a sigh. "That would be nice."

To say I'm confused is an understatement, but as Mum always used to say when the unexpected happened, 'you should never look a gift horse in the mouth'. I'm not about to question him on his decision.

"Great. Any requests on flavour?"

He folds the paper and tosses it on the table before sculling back the last of his drink. "Surprise me." He gives me an odd look, almost as if he's amused by himself, then he kisses me on the cheek. "Have a fun day."

My hand automatically finds the spot his lips brushed against, ghosting across the skin there. I don't know what's going on, and I'm not sure I like it.

"Uh, yeah, you too," I whisper to his back, watching him walk out the door, whistling as he does.

CHAPTER FIFTEEN

HOLDEN

"Hey, look at this." Cami bounds towards me with her phone held out in front of her. "There's a fair on at the preschool." She hands me the phone, resting her hip against the counter and folding her arms. "It's from Darcy," she points out, as if I can't read her name for myself.

"I see that. You gonna go?" I try to play it off like I don't care, when inside every ounce of my being is screaming at me to run to the preschool immediately.

"I think I have to, right? This is the first time she's reached out to me. Plus, her kids will be there." A small smile graces her lips, one I'm sure she's trying to tamp down. "I'll finally get to meet them and practice being the cool aunty."

Only that's not how it will play out, I'm sure. There are no doubts in my mind that Darcy has only messaged because there's no chance of Clay being there, what with it being a Friday. Considering she's warned us both off, I'm not sure she's quite ready to embrace the ex-best-friend-turned-aunty role just yet.

"What do you need to practice for? There some nieces and nephews I don't know about?" I nudge her with my elbow, and she scowls.

"Ha ha, funny guy. One of these days you'll knock some poor unsuspecting gal up and give me what I want."

"Or, and I'm just spit-ballin' here, you could go and have your own kids."

"Oh, I plan on it. I'll have a whole brood of them running around, mark my words. But you're the older sibling, it's your job to go first and teach me what not to do." She sticks her tongue between her teeth as she grins.

"Good to know you have so much faith in me." I ruffle her hair as I go past, and she swipes at me. "What time you heading to this thing? I might tag along."

"Oh, you will, will you?" She grins, as if she's privy to some big secret I know nothing about.

"Yeah, I will. That alright with you?"

"Mmhmm." She nods, dancing over to the jug to pour a coffee. "Why wouldn't it be?"

"You tell me. You're the one acting weird."

With her hands clasped around the warm mug, she spins on her heels to face me. "I'm not acting weird. You are."

"Okay." I draw the word out, grabbing my keys. "If you say so."

She lunges forward, stepping in front of me. "In fact, you've been acting kind of weird ever since you ran into Darcy."

I try to brush her off. "Whatever. I've got to get to work."

"Oh, don't be like that." Her voice takes on a whining lilt. "I'm your little sister. You're meant to share your feelings with me."

I snort. "Uh, I think you have me confused with your make-believe sister. When have I *ever* shared feelings with you?"

She pouts, dropping from her toes to her heels. "I share with you."

Swiping a hand down my face, I level her with a stare. "What *exactly* do you want me to share?"

She sucks her lips between her teeth, her eyes shining as she fights a smile. "How about why you're *so* keen to come to a preschool fair with me?"

"If you don't want me to come, just say and I won't." *That's a lie.*

"That's not what I said, and you know it." She pokes a finger at my chest, then her face turns serious. "Do you have… *feelings* for Darcy?"

I scoff, taking a step away so I can breathe. My jacket suddenly feels tight around my throat, and I yank at the zipper to loosen it. "No. Of course not." Turning my gaze to the floor, I grab at the back of my neck and close my eyes. "Why? Would that be a problem?" The words hang in the air, and I instantly regret them. But when I look up, Cami has a smirk on her face.

"I knew it!"

"What?"

"You *love* her." She hoots, slapping a hand to her thigh. "I bloody well knew it!"

I hold my hands up placatingly. "Wait, I never… huh?" My hand falls to my side, my brow furrowing. "You're okay with it?" I ask tentatively.

She stops her victory dance long enough to slap a hand to my chest. "Are you kidding? My big bro is in love with my best friend! What's not to be okay with?"

"I…" Closing my eyes, I shake my head, letting out a pained laugh. "I don't fucking know, but I had it in my head that you'd hate me if I ever went there."

"Oh, well, if you ever hurt her, I'll slit your throat while you sleep." She smiles sweetly, as if she hasn't just threatened my life. "But that's not going to happen now, is it?"

"Of course not. I'd never hurt her."

"Then it's settled."

"What is?"

She rolls her eyes, looping her arm through mine. "We're going to get her away from Clay, and you're going to marry her, like you should've years ago, and then you'll make me lots of baby nieces and nephews to fawn over."

"Glad to know you've got my whole life planned out for me." I say it like I'm joking, but what she's suggesting sounds bloody perfect. If Darcy'll have me, I'll give her the moon and the stars if that's what she wants. The white picket fence, the garden for the kids to play in, the whole nine yards.

Cami clamps her hand on my shoulder. "The way I see it, it's killing two birds in the bush, or whatever the fuck that saying is. You get the girl and I get my best friend back." She holds her hands up as if comparing weights. "It's a win-win situation as far as I can see."

It might be a win-win for us, but it's certainly not how Clay will see it, and something tells me he's not going to give her up without a fight.

CHAPTER SIXTEEN

DARCY

I see Mum the second she walks through the gate. Her untamed locks fly free in the breeze behind her, and she raises a hand to wave. Her eyes dart around the preschool grounds, taking in all the displays. "This is wonderful, darling," she gushes when she makes it to me. Her hands land softly on my upper arms, and she plants a light-as-air kiss to my cheek.

"The kids have had a great time putting it together."

"Oh, I'm sure. And where are my grandbabies?" She stands on tip-toes, peering over my shoulder. I love how much she dotes on them. Since Dad died, she's been distant, but whenever she sees the children, she's like the mum I remember growing up.

"Oh, they're around somewhere. Bobby is doing the hopscotch. Maybe try there first."

She beams. "Isn't he clever? Running his own stand." Shielding her eyes against the glare of the sun, she scans the area then does a little skip. "Found him!" Then she rushes off without so much as another word.

"Bye." I wave at her retreating back with a chuckle.

"Hey, stranger." Cami grins as she approaches, her arms outstretched. She pulls me in for a hug, which is less awkward than I thought it'd be. It's almost as if the clock has turned back and we're nineteen again, before everything changed. "Was that Diane I just saw running off?"

I follow her gaze. "Yeah, any chance to see the kids." I rock on my heels, my hands sliding into my back pockets.

Cami nods. "How's she doing?" Her voice is quiet, concerned, and it warms my heart.

"It's been difficult. She still misses Dad a lot, some days worse than others. But the kids bring her out of her shell."

She makes a humming sound as she nods. "This looks good." She points at the various stalls spread across the preschool grounds.

"Thanks. It's been a really good turnout, and the weather has played its part." I smile, though inside I'm kicking myself. Is this what we've come to? Talking about the weather?

Cami takes it in stride though, ignoring my ineptitude for holding conversation. She turns her head up to the sky. "It certainly has."

"Mummy!" Molly bounds up to me, wrapping her arms around my legs and almost knocking me over. With a nervous chuckle, I cup the back of her head as she tilts her face upwards. "I founded the most coolest toy in the whole wide world." She flings her arms out wide. "Can I get it please?" She bounces on her toes, her unruly curls dancing about her face.

"I'll come and have a look in a second, okay? I'd, ah, like you to meet someone first." I glance towards Cami, who is watching on with pure adoration in her eyes. Kneeling in front of my daughter, I wrap my arm around her and point at Cami. "This here is one of my oldest and dearest friends. Her name is Cami. And Cami, this is my daughter, Molly."

"Wow." Cami drops to her knees too, coming face-to-face with Molly. "You're so big. How old are you?"

"This many." Molly holds up three fingers, but a fourth keeps popping up that she has to hold down with her other hand. "How old are you?"

Cami chuckles. "I don't have enough fingers to show you, but a lot more than you."

"You remember you met my other friend, Holden, the other day?" Molly nods. "Well, this is his sister."

"Really?" Molly's eyes widen. "I have a brother too. You wanna meet him?"

"I sure do."

"Okay!" Molly darts off through the throngs of children as Cami climbs to her feet.

"She's gorgeous, Darce." There are tears in her eyes, and in mine, and we share a moment, just staring at each other.

"Here he is!" Molly reappears, dragging a disgruntled Bobby behind her. He scowls and pulls his shirt sleeve from her grasp.

"This is my oldest, Bobby. Bobby, this is my friend Cami."

She offers him her hand, and he accepts, shaking solemnly.

"She's Holden's sister!" Molly jumps up and down. "Like me and you!"

This seems to lighten his mood, and he looks at her with renewed interest. "Do you have a motorbike too?"

She laughs. "No, but I do know how to ride one. And if it came down to it, I could probably fix one too."

Bobby's jaw drops. "You could? But you're a girl."

"I am, and girls can do anything boys can, right, Molly?"

Molly nods, her hands falling to her hips. "Yup!"

Bobby doesn't look convinced.

"I hate to break it to you, Bobby, but she's right." Holden steps out of nowhere, clapping a hand on his sister's shoulder. "Cami here would make a pretty good mechanic if she wanted to."

Cami rolls her eyes, as if they've had this conversation a million times before.

"I taught her everything I know. That's what we have to do as big brothers. You know that, right? We look out for our sisters." He winks, ruffling Bobby's hair.

Bobby puffs out his chest, pointing a finger at himself. "I do that. I look after Molly."

"You sure do, bud. I saw at the supermarket that time. I can see Molly looks up to you."

Molly stares at her brother. "Yeah, cos he's taller 'an me."

Holden chuckles, and it does things to my chest. Makes it feel all tight and like I can't get enough air in.

"Exactly." He grins down at her, then turns his gaze to mine, and I swear my heart stops beating for a second or two.

I know it's wrong. I'm a married woman, and he's a ghost from the past, but there's something about watching him interact with my children that makes my heart sing. Clay never speaks to them the way Holden does; like their words hold value.

"Bobby's in charge of the hopscotch, aren't you?" I smooth a hand down his hair, and he nods.

"I am." He toes the ground then peers up at Holden. "Do you want to come see?"

"Sure thing, bud." He looks to me with a wink, taking hold of Bobby's outstretched hand. "Lead the way."

"Huh." Cami watches her brother walking hand-in-hand with my son. "He's actually really good with them."

I can't help but laugh at her. "Why does that surprise you?"

She scrunches her nose. "Because… he's… I don't know. A knucklehead who always has his nose stuck under a bonnet."

"He looked after us, didn't he?"

She rolls her eyes, looping her arm through mine. "I don't think that counts."

"Mummy," Molly whines, tugging on my shirt. "What about my toy?"

"Sorry, sweetheart." I smile down at her and go to take her hand, but she's staring off toward the road. I follow her gaze and almost stumble backwards.

"Daddy!" Molly cries out, running towards him. She flings herself around his legs, but he doesn't pick her up or pull her in for a hug. He just stands there staring back at me, his glassy eyes narrowed.

All the blood in my body seems to rush to my face, the sound deafening as it swooshes in my ears.

Wiping my hands on my jeans, I take a few steps forward. I plaster what I hope is a smile on my face. "Clay, you came," I manage to get out. "I thought you had to work."

"I can see that." His eyes dart behind me, to where I can feel Cami standing.

I turn to her with a pained expression. "Could you, um, take Molly to the toys please?"

She seems to search my gaze before deciding to do as I ask. Dropping to a crouch, she addresses Molly. "How about you show me that toy you wanted, eh?"

Molly peers back to me, and I smile, nodding. "It's okay, sweetheart."

"Okay." She smiles, taking hold of Cami's hand and leading her towards the tables, her mouth going a mile a minute. Poor Cami doesn't know what she's in for.

"What's she doing here?" he demands when I turn back to him.

I gesture to the crowds of people. "It's a preschool fair. Lots of people are here."

"I don't care about anyone else. Why's *she* here?"

I throw my hands up. "I don't know. Maybe she saw it advertised in the paper or one of the signs up around town." I point behind him to a poster hanging on the front gate. "It's not a secret."

His fingers grab hold of my wrist before I even see him move. He pulls me in close. "Don't. Lie. To. Me."

I try to wrench free, but it's no use. "Clay, please." I glance around at the milling people.

"You told me you weren't seeing her anymore."

"I wasn't. I'm not." Tears pool in my eyes, but I blink them away. I will not let him make me cry in front of all these people. "It's a public event, Clay. I can't stop her from being here."

His hand loosens, and I think maybe I've got through to him. "Well maybe it's you who shouldn't be here then."

My shoulders sag and I duck my head. "That's not fair. The children begged me to come." I force myself to meet his stare. "I won't let them down."

"Everything alright here?" a familiar voice asks, and part of me rejoices, while the other part wishes he hadn't chosen this moment to step in.

Clay sucks his teeth, pulling back and dropping his hand. "Everything's fine. Just talking with *my wife*."

He throws an arm around my shoulders, pulling me in tight.

Holden flexes his hands by his side, then holds one out. "Clay, isn't it?"

Clay sneers but takes the offered hand. Veins bulge as they each take a firm grip, neither one letting go. "That's right. And you're that biker, aren't you? Hammond, was it?"

"Holden."

"My mistake."

Attempting to smooth the tension, I rest my hand on Clay's arm. "Why don't I show you around?"

Without taking his eyes from Holden, he agrees, finally letting go of his hand and following me. His hand lands on the base of my spine in a move he hasn't done since we were first dating, and though it would've had my knees wobbling in days gone by, all it does now is make my skin crawl.

Our marriage has never been a particularly happy one, but there was a time when his eyes lit up each time he saw me, and my stomach danced with butterflies whenever he walked into the room. It didn't seem to sour until our vows had been made, and by then it was too late. I was pregnant with no one to turn to. There was nothing I could do but make the best of a bad situation. I found joy in my children and redecorating the house. I learned how to bake, and I can clean a house until it sparkles.

It isn't much, but it was enough to keep me content, to stop me from searching for greener pastures. Now that Holden is back, and Cami too, it's becoming harder to pretend. This isn't the life I had planned. It's certainly not the life I wanted to bring children up in. Somehow along the way I got stuck, like a lost lamb searching for its mother in a ravine. No matter which way I turned, there was no way out, and so I adapted.

But it's not enough anymore. This is not what I signed up for, and my children deserve to live in a safe environment where they don't have to creep around on eggshells for fear they're going to anger their father. Kids are meant to run wild and free with reckless abandon, to hell with the consequences.

I lead Clay around the stalls, pointing out various things the children have made, keeping up the appearance of a normal, happy husband and wife. I do it for the children.

But on the inside, I know things need to change. I can't keep playing the same games and expecting different results. I have to get us out. I just don't know how.

CHAPTER SEVENTEEN

HOLDEN

Once the last of our customers is out the door, we shut up shop and head for the bar. It's been a long week, and after my run-in with Clay this afternoon, I'm ready for a drink.

Cassian is the bar wench tonight. Zeb's on Hannibal duty, following behind on his bike as they head back up north for the weekend. All going well, he'll be there and back within a few hours.

Pulling up a stool, I give Cassian the nod, and he pours a Jack on the rocks. The first mouthful goes down smooth, and I let out a sigh.

"Rough day?" he asks, wiping out a glass with a tea towel before flicking it over his shoulder. If I had to guess, I'd say he's been watching a few too many westerns. Still, it has the desired effect, and I start talking.

"If running into the arsehole husband of the woman I love classifies as a rough day, then yeah. I guess it has been."

Cassian lets out a low whistle. "Think maybe you're barking up the wrong tree, mate?" He shakes his head. "From my experience, getting in bed with a married woman never goes well."

I snort out a laugh. Cassian is nineteen and just as bad as Zeb, who's not much older. When it comes to women, they both think they're some sort of Casanova, when really, they wouldn't have the first clue how to handle a woman if she gave them a second glance.

"What'd your dad say when he caught you?" I snigger, downing the rest of my glass and sliding it across for a refill.

Cassian frowns. "It wasn't my… Oh." He grins, pointing a finger in my face. "I walked into that one." He pours a splash of Jack into my glass and pushes it towards me. I eye the glass then him, until he relents and adds another finger.

"You lot make it way too easy."

"Who's easy?" Matiu parks himself beside me, Barb taking the seat next to him.

"We all know you are," I say to him, giving Barb a nod.

"He's not wrong." She leans across the bar. "I'll grab a cider please."

Matiu snorts and tilts his head in agreeance. "It's the only way to be." He reaches behind and slaps Barb on the arse. "Right, babe?"

She gives him the side-eye, but her lips are turned up into a grin. The easiness between them has me thinking of Darcy and how it's always felt so natural between us. There was no awkward shit like there is now, and I miss it.

There's a loud holler, and I turn to see Jericho and Sam walking in. He makes his way to Stubbs sitting at one of the leaners, while Sam heads straight for Barb. They hug, like they haven't spent all day in the salon together, then Sam takes a seat beside her. Matiu is forgotten as their heads practically join, deep in discussions. No doubt it's more wedding talk.

"I hear you had a run-in with old douche canoe today." Matiu swipes his thumb across his nose. "Can't believe the guy is still standing."

"Believe me, it wasn't easy walking away. I think Darcy could tell something was brewing, because she got between us before anything could happen." I shake my head then knock back my whiskey. "Of course, he preened like the fucking peacock he is, thinking he's won." I tap the bar for Cassian, and he pours another for me and one for Matiu.

"Well." He draws out the word, and I silence him with a glare.

"Don't fucking start."

"I'm just saying, if she's still going home with him, I think he's won." He pulls out a cigarette and lights up, handing it to Barb before lighting his own. "We need to show him what's what."

"And how do you propose we do that?"

He shrugs, huffing out a ring of smoke. "You're the ideas man, not me. You figure it out." He takes a drink. "Whatever you decide on, you know I've got your back."

"Hold up." Barb swivels in her seat. "Got your back for what?" She points a finger at me. "You better not be getting him into trouble. I'd like at least one of his hands in working order, thank you very much."

I almost snort my whiskey out my nose at that. "Sounds like you might need to get some practice in, bro. Your old lady's complaining about your technique."

He rears back. "What? Nah, my hand's all goods." He waggles the fingers of his uninjured hand.

Barb wraps her arms around his neck, pulling him in for a kiss. "You've got mad skills, babe." She cranes her neck to look at me. "I just meant he'd better not lose the use of *both* hands. One needs to stay in action." She smirks, and I can't help but chuckle. Matiu certainly knows how to pick them. I don't think I've met anyone else who could put up with his shit and give it back as good as she gets.

"See? I got more skills in my pinkie than you do in your whole hand, man."

"Whatever you need to tell yourself, bro."

"Seriously, though. What are you getting him into?" Barb cocks her head to the side, her hand falling to her hip. Sam swivels on her seat, giving me her attention too.

Well shit.

I rake a hand through my hair, then toss back the rest of my drink. "There's this girl."

Sam grins, and Barb hoots out a laugh. "Isn't there always?"

"Oh, this isn't just any girl," Matiu pipes up, clapping a hand on my shoulder. "This is the one that got away."

Sam grimaces. "She's with someone else?"

"Not just *with* him. She *married* the prick and had two kids with him." He points at Sam. "Kinda like you and Dante, only without the crotch goblins."

She holds her hands up. "That was out of my control."

Matiu snorts. "So was this."

I shoot him a look. "He got her pregnant, so they got married," I clarify. "And then once they were married, he started laying into her."

Sam gasps, and she stands from her seat, gripping onto Barb's arm. "He hits her?" It's close to home for her, I know. Her father married her off to Dante Costello to pay off his debts, and she was kept under lock and key until she managed to cut loose and find her way here.

"Among other things."

Barb slaps Matiu in the chest. "And you knew about this?"

He flinches away, a look of pure shock on his face. "Hey, what was that for? I'm not the one hitting her." He rubs at the spot she whacked.

"What about the kids?" Sam asks, a frown creasing her brow.

"As far as I know, it's only Darcy he takes it out on, not the kids."

"For now," she mutters under her breath, then gives me an apologetic look.

"My thoughts exactly."

"Shit."

"Yeah." I close my eyes and see his hand gripping her arm at the fair. No doubt she will have faced his wrath when they made it home. Another bruise to add to the collection. My fists clench at my sides knowing I only made things worse by being there.

"We could bring her here," Sam suggests. "I could make up some beds in the meeting room and you lot can meet out here until we sort it out."

"Thanks, Sam, but I don't think this is the place to be bringing kids." I gesture to the bar and the empty bottles already piling up.

"Nah, he wants to play happy families with her anyway." Matiu nudges my ribs with his elbow, making a kissy face. "Ain't that right, loverboy?"

This time it's me jostling him with an elbow. I mean, he's right, but I'm not about to admit it. Even if I manage to convince her to leave, it's not like she's going to jump straight into another relationship. Hell, I wouldn't blame her if she wanted nothing to do with another man again. It'd cut me up, but I'd understand. All I can really focus on for right now, is keeping her and those kids safe.

"I'm more concerned about getting her out of there alive."

Matiu nods solemnly, and I instantly regret saying it. It wasn't so long ago we lost Tony in the fight to save Sam. Matiu had been one of the guys on the ground that day. He took a bullet to the hand trying to give Jericho the time he needed to get inside. Tony hadn't made it out alive.

"Sorry, bro, I wasn't thinking."

"What?" He frowns, then quirks a brow. "Oh, nah, man, you're all good. It just makes me angry, you know?"

"Believe me, I know. If it was as simple as going up to the house and dragging her out of there, I would, but think what that would do to the kids."

"Yeah, you have to be careful around children." Sam glances toward Jericho across the room with Stubbs. They're deep in conversation, but his eyes always seem to find hers, no matter who he's talking to. It's like they have some weird sixth sense of each other. "The things we see as kids can make or break us."

Ain't that the truth? Cami and I were the lucky ones; born to great parents who showed us nothing but love. But Darcy, though she'd had a loving home, it had been her father's sudden death that pushed her into the arms of Clay Ferriman. He'd shown up at the right time, full of promises for a girl whose mother was so lost in her grief she could barely function anymore.

Even our leader had his childhood demons, and they framed the very being he is today; a protector. Jericho had the upbringing of nightmares. An alcoholic, abusive father who used his fists on his family. Jeremiah Lawson is currently serving a lifetime sentence in Paparua Prison for killing his wife. If it were up to Jericho he'd be serving double time for the hand he had in his sister's death too. He hadn't been the one to tie the rope around her neck, but witnessing their father beat their mother to a pulp was the reason she turned to methamphetamines.

Sam's father was a gambler who married her off to pay his debts, and Matiu was left on a doorstep when he was only a few days old. No note left with him, just a baby wrapped in a blanket and tucked into a cardboard box. Luckily, Celeste Kawiti was a kind woman who took him in and gave him a home.

We're all the product of our childhoods, and there's no way in hell I'm going to give those kids anything else to be scared of. I won't take them from their home without a solid plan, and though it pains me to leave her with him, I won't do a damn thing without Darcy's approval first. I'm not going to be another man storming into her life and telling her what to do.

CHAPTER EIGHTEEN

DARCY

The usually soft wool of my cardigan scrapes across my tender flesh as I pull it on. Last night, Clay showed me just how much he hated seeing me with Cami and Holden. He was like a man possessed, using his fists, his belt, and the tip of a lit cigarette. The trifecta. It's the worst beating he's doled out in a long time, and it's more than cemented my decision. I can't keep doing this. If I stay, he'll end up killing me.

My reflection in the mirror is a pitiful sight. He doesn't normally go for the face, but I guess in his fit of rage, he lost control. At least, that's what he told me after while he apologised profusely.

I touch a tentative fingertip to the deep red lump above my eye. I hate to think how much worse it would've been if my glasses hadn't taken the brunt of the blow. As it is, it's going to take a lot of make-up to cover.

I do the best I can with concealer and foundation, then let my hair fall loose around my face. It'll have to do.

Clay slinks into the room, his eyes downcast as he shucks off his pyjamas and pulls on jeans and a shirt. He sits on the bed to tie his boots before finally looking at me. His eyes narrow on my made-up face. "You going somewhere?"

I fold my arms across my chest. "I could ask you the same thing."

"I'm going in to work, getting a head start on loading the truck for Monday. What are *you* doing?" He stands, moving towards me slowly, as if afraid I'll bolt. His hand reaches out for my chin, tilting my head upwards and side-to-side. "And why've you got all this shit on your face?"

I slap his hand away. "I'm going to the store to pick up some milk and bread. And this *shit* is covering what you did last night." I practically spit the words in his face, and he recoils. In all our years of marriage, I've never spoken to him this way.

"Right then." He clears his throat a few times then swipes a hand across his lips. "Okay." He turns towards the door then stops, his fingers tapping on the frame. "There and straight back," he says, as if he still has any control over me.

I don't bother to answer him, and when he realises I have nothing to say, he sighs then stalks from the room.

Once the front door slams and I hear his truck pull down the drive, I bustle down the hall to where the children are watching Saturday morning TV. I clap my hands twice then switch it off. "Right, you two. Time to get dressed. We're going out."

At the store, I load our basket up with a few necessities, all the while scanning the store for any signs of Holden. We walk up and down each aisle a handful of times before I resign myself to the fact he's not here. I don't know why I thought he'd show up at the same time as the other week. It was stupid really. He has a life and no need to work to a strict schedule like me.

We head up to the checkout and pay. The girl behind the counter is young, maybe fifteen, and I'm almost positive she's the same one from last time. On a whim, I hang by the counter until she's finished with the next customer.

"Excuse me," I say, leaning over the counter and plastering a smile on my face. "This might be odd, but you don't happen to know Holden Hart, do you? He's one of the Hellhounds?"

She scrunches her nose then shakes her head. "No, sorry. I only started here two weeks ago." She shrugs, and I thank her before gathering the kids and walking out the door to the car. I load our bags into the car and buckle the kids into their seats, then close the door and stand there, peering around the quiet streets. I suppose I could try Lawson's Lugs.

"Um, hi." Someone taps me on the shoulder, and I turn to see a slender woman with long blonde hair. "I couldn't help overhear you're looking for Holden?" She hooks her thumb over her shoulder. "I was in the other checkout."

"Oh, yeah. Do you know him?" I take in her svelte figure. There's a pang in my chest as I realise she probably knows him on a level I've only ever dreamed of.

She slings her bag over her shoulder. "Yeah, he works with my partner. Jericho Lawson?" She says it like a question, as if his name should mean something to me, but it doesn't. She waves her hand through the air dismissively. "Anyway, he's out on a job with him, but he should be back mid-afternoon. Do you want to wait at my place?"

"Oh, um…" I glance at the children peering out at me. "I can't. Need to get them back home." I brush a wayward strand of hair behind my ear then quickly pull it back when I see her staring. "Uh, thanks though." I back towards the car, fumbling for the handle.

Her hand brushes against my arm. "Please don't go, I can… I can get a message to him if you like."

"Um." I don't know who this girl is or why she's being so nice to me, but it's throwing me off kilter. "I don't want to trouble you."

"It's no trouble." She rummages in her bag and pulls out a pen and notebook. "Here. Write what you need to say, and I'll make sure he sees it." She smiles, though her gaze is probing, like she can see more than I want to show.

With the notebook resting on the bonnet of my car, I quickly scrawl out a message.

Holden,

If you and Cami are still willing to help me, I'm ready to let you. I've done a lot of thinking over these past few weeks, and you're right, I do deserve better, and so do my kids.

I can get us packed up and ready to go on Tuesday while he's at work and the children are at preschool. We'll wait by the gates at 3pm.

Yours
Darcy

P.S. I'm glad you came back

"Um, here. Thank you." I tear the page from the book and fold it in half before handing it to her. She stuffs it in her bag with a nod.

"I'll make sure he gets it as soon as he's back." She offers her hand. "I'm Sam."

"Darcy." Her hands are warm, the skin smooth. She has short acrylic nails painted dark red, and a thin gold band on her index finger.

"I hope this isn't crossing a line, but if you ever need somewhere to go or someone to talk to, I work at A Cut Above, the hair salon. And if I'm not there, I live in the apartment above Lawson's Lugs." She points down the road. "I'm a pretty good listener."

Tears prick my eyes at the kindness of this stranger, and I realise again how much I've missed out on by being stuck at home day in and day out. A simple conversation with a stranger, making friends, having someone to turn to. All things I took for granted before marrying Clay.

"Thank you," I say. "I'll keep that in mind."

She watches me climb into the car and waves as we pull away. I switch the radio on and wind the window down, letting the breeze blow my hair about my face. And I smile, leaning my head against the back of the seat. My shoulders no longer feel as though they're carrying the weight of the world, and my head feels clear for the first time in a long time. I'm getting us out, and we're going to be free.

CHAPTER NINETEEN

HOLDEN

We pull up outside what appears to be an empty warehouse in the industrial area of town. Across the road is a lot with four large grain silos, a fleet of transport trucks, and an engineering firm. All three places are closed for the weekend.

Jericho leads the way up the path and through the wire gates to the scrapyard next door. A man wearing a white hardhat walks out from the office, wiping his hands on a rag then tossing it over his shoulder. Jericho hands him a fifty, then we wheel our bikes in and park them up beside a bale of wires. We slip back out on foot towards the warehouse.

From the front, there's nothing special about the place. Corrugated iron sheets wrap around the building with one lone window to the left of a small PA door. No lights are on inside.

"I don't understand. What're we doing here?" I follow him round to the back where there's a large open bay and a truck backed up with a ramp leading across.

Jericho holds his finger to his lips, pressing himself against the side of the building.

Across the way, I see the same SUV that met with Hannibal the other day, and the meathead who drove Mr. Takanawa leans his back against the car door, his feet crossed at the ankles.

"What's going on?" I whisper. "Is it Hannibal?"

Jericho shakes his head then points two fingers from his eyes to the bay. I inch closer to get a better look. He grabs hold of my arm, giving me a look that warns me to be careful. I nod once then move in.

Mr. Takanawa is standing on the raised floor of the warehouse, speaking on the phone. A guy with a cap pulled low over his face is rolling a sack barrow loaded with unmarked boxes off the truck and across the ramp. He makes several trips before handing Mr. Takanawa a clipboard, which he signs. The guy tips his hat, then closes up the back of the truck, glancing around the otherwise empty lot.

"Son of a bitch," I hiss beneath my breath as I get a glimpse of his face. What the fuck is Clay doing here?

I press myself into the wall as he struts round to the driver's door and climbs in. The truck starts up with a rumble, and as he pulls out of the lot, I'm able to see the writing on the side. *Lyman's Seeds.* Only that wasn't seeds he was unloading.

We wait as the roller door squeals on its tracks and the SUV pulls up beside the docking bay. Mr. Takanawa makes his way down the ramp, his short legs moving in a half-run half-skip fashion.

Once they're gone, I turn to Jericho with a raised brow. "What is this?"

He folds his arms across his chest. "That's what we're here to find out." He saunters past me, leaping up onto the loading bay.

"Isn't this Hannibal's place?" I ask, following him up.

"It is, but like you, I don't know that I trust the guy. This way we can make sure we're helping the right people." He grabs hold of the padlock at the base of the door. "You know how to open one of these?"

I laugh. "If that's why you asked me here, you picked the wrong guy. I'm a gearhead like you, mate. I don't know the first thing about picking locks."

"Good thing I brought someone else then." He whistles, and Zeb darts out from the other side of the building. He pumps his legs and leaps up onto the bay with a goofy grin.

"How's your sister?" he asks, dodging the hand flying towards his face with a laugh. "Touchy." He cracks his knuckles as Jericho steps aside. From his back pocket, he pulls a leather pouch and drops it to the ground. Holding what looks like two thin strips of wire, he jiggles them inside the lock until it clicks open. "Ta da," he sings, stepping back and admiring his handy work.

Jericho grabs the handle and lifts, the doors emitting another loud screech. He points to Zeb. "Stay out here and keep watch."

Zeb gives a salute and jumps down to the ground, slipping into the shadows once more. I follow Jericho in, pulling the door halfway closed.

Inside, boxes are stacked along one wall, and in the centre is a line of pallets with two rows of wooden crates, stacked three high.

"I don't like the look of those."

"Neither do I." Jericho circles the front pallet with trepidation. "Find me something to jack them open with." He steps onto the pallet and drags one of the crates from the top and down to the floor.

There's an office in the back corner with a window overlooking the warehouse. Beneath that is a long cabinet. I scour the cupboards and shelves then move on to the next room. It's a small bathroom that looks as though it hasn't seen a cleaner in years. To the right of that is another office, then a workshop space. I find a crowbar lying between two jacks and swipe it up, jogging back to Jericho.

He jimmies the lid off and it falls to the floor with a clunk. Nestled amongst wood shavings, are four swords with ornate handles.

"The fuck?" I reach in and grasp hold of one, pulling it from its sheath with a satisfying shick sound. "Who uses swords these days?"

Jericho points to an engraving on the side of the hilt. It has some sort of stamp and a number and date below. "Collectors, by the look of that." He eyes the remaining pallets. "I'm going to check another."

I swing the blade back and forth a few times like a five-year-old boy playing pirates. The way it wooshes through the air is almost hypnotic, and I can see the appeal of having one.

"More of the same," Jericho says, crouching beside another open crate. "He was telling the truth."

"So Hannibal is like an antiques dealer or some shit? I don't buy it." I sheath the sword and place it back in the crate, and as I do, the shavings shift, revealing another layer. "Hold up." Carefully placing each sword on the floor, I push the shavings aside, letting out a whistle.

"What is it?"

My fingers curl around the cool metal handle, and I heft the handgun into the air. "*This* makes more sense."

Jericho does the same to his crate and holds up yet another handgun, this one slightly larger. "Shit."

"Shit alright. Who you think's buying these here in Brookhaven?"

"I don't know. But I don't like it. In my experience, guns go hand-in-hand with drugs, or worse." He places the weapons back into their crate, packing the wood shavings carefully around them. "I've seen enough. Let's get out of here."

I follow his lead, repacking the crate and hefting it back onto the pile, when there's a loud whistle from outside and the sound of tyres crunching over gravel.

"We got company," I hiss, darting behind the pallet.

"Back there." Jericho points to the office, and with our bodies hunched, we move quickly and silently into the cramped space.

Footsteps. The roller door squealing.

"Mr. Takanawa?" It's Clay. "Anybody here?" More footsteps, then, "It's all clear."

Two men follow him in; one short and squat, wearing a backwards cap, the other tall with a beer belly and thinning hair. Clay pulls the door down behind them.

"This way." He leads them past the pallets, along the wall of cardboard boxes. Their footsteps echo in the large space, making them sound as if they're right outside the door.

There's a sniff, then a scraping of cardboard, followed by the thud of a box hitting the ground. "Just these back ones. I can't be drawing attention, you see." He sniffs again, then a box cutter is run across the taped lid.

"What're you playin' at?" one asks, his voice gritty like he smokes a pack a day.

"Just wait." There's amusement in Clay's voice, and I edge toward the window to get a look. He's squatting by an open box, pulling out a box of ammo. He tears the lid off and holds up a brass shell.

"I told you it was a waste of time." The tall guy whacks the other in the arm. "Still the same old Clay out to make a quick buck."

"Nah, it's not like that." Clay stands, his hand outstretched. "Just look." He twists the lead end off the shell casing and holds both out to them.

The short guy grins, elbowing his mate in the ribs. "Told you he'd be good for it." He licks his pinkie and shoves it in the end of the casing before bringing it to his lips.

"Purest angel dust you'll find." He holds it out to the tall guy, but he shakes his head.

"I don't partake in what I sell. Bad for business."

Clay shrugs, tipping a small amount of the powder onto the back of his hand and snorting it. "Suit yourself."

"Well?"

The short one smiles a toothy grin. "It's good."

"How much can you supply?"

Clay slaps his hand on one of the boxes. "There's these three boxes, with 18 cases of shells in each. I can bring more in a fortnight." He runs his tongue along his teeth. "If the price is right."

"I'm sure we can come to an arrangement." They each grab a box and carry them back outside, the roller door squealing into place.

We wait until we hear the car pull away before stepping out of the office. "Fucking knew it." I rake a hand through my hair. I thought the arsehole's eyes looked primed when I saw him yesterday. There's no denying it, whether she wants my help or not, I have to get her out of there.

"You know that guy?"

I nod. "Clay Ferriman. Scum of the fucking earth."

Jericho paces the floor. "Where the fuck is he getting it from?"

"Beats me. He was never the sharpest tool in the shed. Ain't no way he's cooking it himself. He has to have a partner." I toe the nearest pallet. "You don't think Hannibal…?" I leave it hanging in the air.

"I don't know, but I'm going to find out." Jericho pulls out his phone and punches in a number. "We need to talk."

CHAPTER TWENTY

DARCY

Clay was in an oddly good mood all weekend. He didn't raise a hand to me again, and even took the children and me to the park for a picnic lunch on Sunday. It was nice, if not a little eerie. I couldn't help waiting for the next mood swing to hit, but it never did.

It occurs to me he could have a bit on the side putting a smile on his face. Perhaps that's where he was all day Saturday and why he returned looking like the cat who got the cream.

It should bother me, but it doesn't. In fact, it makes my plan so much easier if there *is* someone in the side-lines ready to take my place. Though things are rarely that easy when it comes to Clay. It's more likely he had a win on the pokies and bought himself something flashy to show off around the smoko room. Something to make him seem more important than he is.

Whatever it was, it made our weekend surprisingly pleasant for a change, and in a way, I'm glad the children got to have one last family outing that didn't end in tears.

As soon as he's out the door, I hurry the children into their preschool clothes and pack their bags with a spare change of clothes, snacks, and a jacket in case the weather turns, as well as an extra pair of shoes. We race out the door in record time, and I'm waving them goodbye before I even realise.

My stomach churns with nervous energy as I make my final journey back to the place I've lived the past five years. I won't call it a home, because it's never felt like that. Not even in the early days.

Once I'm back, I reverse the car up to the front door, ready to load our bags. I've been thinking about it non-stop all weekend, and I think I've narrowed it down to the bare necessities, plus a few home comforts for the children; favourite books and toys, and the crocheted blankets my mum made them when they were born.

I start in Molly's room, tenderly touching a finger to the mobile still hanging above her bed. Pulling a small suitcase down from the cupboard, I load it with several changes of underwear, pyjamas, and clothes. I add in her hairbrush and toothbrush, then crawl under her bed to retrieve the pink teddy bear she's had since birth. Sitting on the floor in front of her bookshelf, I trail a finger over the spines until I find the ones she'll want. The ones she asks for every night. The last thing I grab is her fluffy dressing gown and slippers. With arms loaded, I stagger out to the car and throw them into the boot.

It took longer than I meant it to, and I only have an hour before Clay is due home from work for lunch. So it doesn't look suspicious, I move the car to my usual spot in front of the garage before heading into Bobby's room.

I try not to linger this time. No need to be sentimental about a room when I'm taking the most important things with me; the children.

His room is easier in a way. That little bit older than his sister, he has less he's attached to. Even with him being a difficult baby, he never really held onto things the way Molly did and still does. She can't sleep without her teddy bear and a myriad pillows and cushions surrounding her, while he prefers the one flat pillow and nothing else. My no-frills baby, that's what he is.

I have his case packed and loaded into the car with five minutes to spare. In the kitchen, I fill the jug and set it to boil while I busy myself preparing an omelette for Clay's lunch. Diced onion, sliced ham, grated cheese, and mushrooms sit on the chopping board, and the minute I see his truck pull into the drive, I turn the pan to high and get started. By the time he's taken his boots off and stepped inside, I'm adding the finishing touches before folding it in half and depositing it on a plate for him.

"You seen my hat anywhere? It's not in the truck." He trudges in, rubbing his hand back and forth through his mussed hair.

"You might've left it in the car after the picnic," I offer as I stir his coffee. "I'll check for you."

"No rush." His hands curl around my waist from behind, the stale smell of cigarette smoke on his breath wafting up my nose. "Smells good," he says, planting a brief kiss to my cheek before heading for the table. He sits, his legs spread wide as he waits for me to serve him.

I place the plate of food and his extra strong coffee to get through the afternoon in front of him, then step back, leaning against the counter. He nods his approval then digs in, barely taking a breath between bites.

When he's done, he pushes the plate away and leans back in his seat. "You're not eating?" he asks, letting out a belch from the corner of his mouth.

"Oh, I'm not hungry," I say, patting my stomach. "I feel a little off today." My nerves are strung too tight to even stomach the idea of eating food. *Only a few more hours until I'm free,* I remind myself.

He eyes me as I clear his plate away and wipe out the frying pan. "Maybe I should take the rest of the day off to look after you."

"No!" I blurt out without thinking. "I mean, thank you, but it's not necessary. I'm sure you're busy at work." I force a smile to my lips. "I might just take a nap before I collect the children. I'm sure I'll feel right as rain after a sleep."

He cranes his neck, glancing around the room to the laundry basket of clothes to be folded, the unwashed breakfast dishes, and last night's coffee cup still sitting beside his chair. In my haste to set the ball in motion, I'd neglected my chores. A rookie mistake.

"Looks like that's all you've been doing anyway." He raises his brow, taking a large gulp of his coffee then letting out a sigh. "I don't ask for much, love. A clean house and food on the table when I come home." He holds his hands out in a small shrug, and my cheeks flush red with anger. But I bite it down and move towards the living room and gather up the empty cup.

"I know, I'm sorry. I'll get them done before I rest. I promise."

I fill the sink with hot, sudsy water and get to work on the first of my chores. Anything to avoid having to face him. I'm no good at deception. He's always been able to see through me.

He downs his coffee and stomps down to the bathroom, and I let out a breath of relief. My hands are shaking, whether from nerves or adrenalin, I'm not sure. It takes all my effort to keep them steady enough to get through the dishes without incident. I drape a tea towel over the pile, leaving them to drip dry for a few minutes while I make a start on the laundry.

The toilet flushes, and Clay takes a seat in his recliner, rolling a cigarette. He pulls something from his pocket and sprinkles it over the tobacco before licking the edges of the paper and sealing it shut. He strikes a match and holds it to the tip, drawing in a breath and closing his eyes. "Things are looking up for us, Darce." He grins, leaning forward, his elbows braced on his knees.

"They are?" I ask, wondering where this is going. Maybe it has something to do with the good mood he's been in lately.

"Oh yeah." The cigarette glows red as he takes another drag then arcs his hands through the air like a rainbow. "Real good."

"Did you get that promotion?"

He snorts. "Better. I got a little something going on the side. Something that'll make us rich." He points his cigarette at me, his eyes glazing over. "It's a sure thing."

"Oh? That's great, Clay." I smile, playing along. "I'm proud of you."

Clay lounges back in his seat, a drowsy smile on his face. "I told you I'd be something."

I glance at the clock. "You're going to be late for work if you don't get going."

He laughs, waggling his finger at me. "That's funny, love." He takes one last drag before stubbing it out in the ashtray. Pushing up from the chair, he swaggers over to me, grabbing my chin roughly and angling my face up to his. His lips press into mine, his hand grabbing hold of my arse and squeezing.

"Clay," I caution, pulling away.

"You're no fun anymore, Darce." He frowns. "We used to have fun, didn't we?"

Once upon a time, yes. He would shower me with compliments and surprise me with flowers. We would go out on dates and make plans for our future together. It had been good back then. A dream come true; or so

I'd thought. He'd promised to protect me, and instead became the person I needed protection from.

"Yes, Clay," I humour him. "We did. I'll try harder."

He grins. "That's my girl." Then he turns for the door.

I listen for the sound of the truck starting up, but it doesn't come. Instead, there's the click of a car door, followed by feet crunching on the gravel.

His hat.

Shit.

My stomach lurches, my chest pulled tight, squeezing the breath out of me. A roar of anger comes from outside, and then the boot slams shut.

A high-pitched sound rings in my ears as I blindly stagger down the hall. "No, no, no, no, no," I chant, searching in vain for somewhere to hide.

Clay comes thundering back into the house, and something hits the wall.

"What the fuck is this?" he demands, and I glance back to see the kids' clothes and toys explode out across the floor.

I back down the hall, my hands held up as if they can stop what will surely come next. "Please, Clay."

"Please what? Let you go? Let you run off with *my* children?" He laughs sardonically as he storms towards me, grabbing hold of my wrists and throwing me to the floor. "You're not going anywhere."

Chapter Twenty-One

Holden

"Come on, Cami." I drum my hands on the steering wheel, waiting for her to get her shit together. Preschool finishes in fifteen minutes, and I don't want Darcy to have to wait a second. When I showed Cami the letter, she'd danced around the living room for a solid twenty minutes before we sat down and made some plans. We'd spent the weekend setting up the spare room with bunk beds we found at the second-hand dealers, a set of drawers I borrowed from Mum and Dad, and a few new toys to make them feel welcome. No matter how rough things are at home, it is still going to be a daunting thing for them to up and leave, and I want them to feel safe here.

Cami even opted to switch out her queen bed for two singles and emptied out a couple of drawers for Darcy. I'm under no illusions that this is the time for professing my undying love for her, and putting her up with Cami makes the most sense. They were best friends for years, and I have no doubt it's a friend she's going to need right now.

"Sorry!" Cami dashes out the door and throws herself into the front seat. "Nervous wee."

I shake my head. "Too much info, sis."

"I don't think you realise how huge this is." She grabs hold of my bicep with both hands. "She's leaving him and she's coming home."

"I know." I can't help but grin.

"It's all because of you, you know."

"No it's not. You went out there and got the ball rolling."

"Pssh. I never would've gone out there if you hadn't given me the kick in the arse I needed." She gives me a sidewards glance. "Thank you, by the way." Bouncing in her seat, she pulls her seatbelt on. "I'm getting my best friend back!"

I chuckle, pulling the car out onto the road. I had to borrow the one we keep at Hellhounds for when we need to be inconspicuous. Somehow, I don't think Darcy would appreciate me showing up on my bike.

"I feel like *Bonnie and Clyde*, don't you? We just need this car to be topless and a couple of scarves on our heads." She cackles, and I shake my head.

"Pretty sure you're thinking of *Thelma and Louise*."

"Am I?" She scrunches her nose. "Whatever. We're like outlaws about to run the biggest job of our lives."

I snort out another laugh. "You watch far too much TV. Aren't you meant to be looking for another job?"

"Stop harshing my vibe, bro." She flicks on a pair of sunglasses and leans her head against the back of the seat. "I'm like excited, and anxious, and also kinda hungry all at once." She bolts upright. "Ooh! We should get doughnuts!"

"We're not on a stake-out. Jesus." I jest, but hearing her non-stop babble is managing to calm my nerves. I keep worrying that she won't be there. That she will have changed her mind.

"I'm sorry, I thought doughnuts were an everyday food, not only for cops on the job." She rolls her eyes dramatically. "Apparently a girl can't have cravings."

"Jesus, Cami, I'll buy you a fucking doughnut later, okay? We don't have time to stop right now." I glance at the blinking clock on the dashboard. Two fifty-five.

"It's up there." She points at the same time I switch on the indicator.

"I know. I was here the other day too, remember?"

She cranes her neck, lowering her glasses as she glares at me. "Do *you* need a doughnut? Talk about hangry."

"I'm not…" I huff out a breath. "I'm not *hangry*. I just want to get there on time."

She holds her hands up, palms out. "Okay. Chill. We're here." She's unbuckling her seatbelt before I even stop the car. "I don't see her."

I don't either. Pushing the door open, I step out into the cool air and search up and down the road. No sign of her car.

Shit.

She's had second thoughts. I knew it. I knew it was too good to be true. Everything was falling in to place too easily.

"Wait." Cami slaps her hand on the roof of the car. "Over there." I follow where she's pointing to see the faded blue Toyota Corolla that's been parked in her drive every time I've gone past.

A grin forms on my lips as I shut the door and hurry across to the gates. Cami takes my hand, squeezing it, and I squeeze back. *This is it*.

The car slows as it approaches, and I know instantly that something isn't right. There are two people in the car, one hunched against the door, and the other staring out at me with beady eyes.

Clay Ferriman.

"Oh my God!" Cami gasps, her hand flying to her lips. "What's he done to her?"

My jaw clenches, and I speak through my teeth. "I don't know, but he's going to pay for it." I shake my hand free of hers, fists already forming as I stalk towards the car.

"Holden, no!" Cami lunges for my hand, tugging me backwards as a bell chimes from the school across the road. Screams and laughter fill the air as children file out. "Not here. Not now."

Clay pulls the car to a stop, clambering out and slamming the door behind him. He walks across the road with a swagger, his tongue dragging across his teeth. "Sorry to derail your plans, *Hellhound,* but Darcy decided to stay." He shoves his thumbs into the loops of his jeans, rocking on his heels.

"Looks more like you did the deciding for her," I seethe, my jaw tight and hands itching to wrap around his throat.

He glances over his shoulder. "She just needed a little reminding is all."

"You're a fucking pig," Cami spits from behind me. "Only a coward picks on someone smaller."

He rakes his eyes up and down her petite frame. "Someone like you?"

I step in front of her, my palm pressed into his chest. "Someone like me."

Clay juts his chin, stepping right into my space. "Keep sniffing around my wife and that just might happen." He eyeballs me, and I give it right back. No fucking way will I be the first to back down.

Cami moves to my side. "People are watching. I suggest you get out of here if you don't want them knowing what kind of a scumbag you are."

He drags his eyes away, sneering at her. "You first."

"Come on." She tugs on my arm, and reluctantly, I follow.

"We can't leave her with him."

"We won't. I'm going to call Topher."

CHAPTER TWENTY-TWO

DARCY

Molly won't stop looking at me with sad, confused eyes. I've tried to shield her from this side of our life as much as possible, and though I have my suspicions she knows more than she lets on, I think this is the first time she's piecing it all together. She keeps reaching her chubby fingers out every time a tear slides from the swelling around my eye, as if she wants to wipe it away but doesn't know if she should.

Bobby has been quiet all afternoon, which is unusual on a preschool day. He's barely said two words, and he can't seem to look at me. All through dinner he pushed his food around his plate until Clay told him to knock it off.

I wish I could wave a magic wand and make it all better. I'd give anything for them to have a normal upbringing, away from all the anger and the hurt. I'd gladly stay and take my punishments if it meant they could be free from all this. I worry what it's doing to their impressionable minds. Children are like sponges, soaking up everything they see and hear, and I'd hate for them to think the way Clay treats us is 'normal'.

Pushing up from the table, I hobble to the sink with my plate. Bobby brings his up too, and without a word, he takes mine and rinses it for me. His pudgy hand finds mine, and he wraps his fingers around my own before walking away.

I swallow back the lump in my throat, my chin tucked into my chest. He brings the other plates up and does the same with them, then takes his sister's hand. "Come on, Molly-moo, time for your bath."

"But Mummy does it," she whimpers.

"I'm doing it tonight," he says. "Big brothers have to look after their sisters, you know."

"They do?"

"Sure. It's the rules."

"Oh." She draws it out, and I can picture her staring up at him with awe. "Okay then."

Once they're gone, I move into the living room and curl up on the couch, my head resting on a cushion. I close my eyes, trying to rid myself of the thumping headache I've had since I woke up on the floor this afternoon. It pulses in time with my heartbeat; a constant rhythm that doesn't let up.

It's the first time Clay has left me where I lay after a beating. The first time he didn't apologise after or try to make me comfortable. When I came to, he was sitting across from me in the recliner, his hands steepled over his knees. He had a cigarette dangling from his lips, a long line of ash ready to fall to the floor at any moment. His eyes, still glazed and stony, bore holes in my head. He didn't say a word, didn't move a muscle, just sat there, staring at me.

My eyes had slid closed several times as I lapsed into unconsciousness. I don't know how long I lay like that, but the next time I awoke, I was in the car and the children were in the backseat. The realisation that I'd missed my window was too much to take, and though I'd tried to hide it, tears ran slowly down my cheeks, soaking the collar of my blouse.

I don't know if I have it in me to try again.

"Who the bloody hell is this?" Clay calls out from the kitchen table, and it's then I notice the car lights shining through the window.

There's a knock on the door, and the chair legs scrape across the floor as Clay stands. He gives me a pointed stare. "Not a fucking word," he hisses.

I don't bother answering him, just close my eyes and pretend I'm anywhere but here.

"Sergeant Grayson. What can I do for you?" Clay's voice booms, and I push myself up to a sitting position.

"Might I have a word with your wife?"

Oh no.

"What for? What's this about?"

"I received a distressing call regarding your wife's safety, and I'd like to talk with her."

"My wife's *safety*? That's ridiculous. She's fine." His voice has risen an octave, and even I can tell he sounds guilty.

"All the same, I'd like to see for myself." The door snicks closed, and Topher Grayson walks in, removing his hat. He's taller than I remember and broader too, but his face still looks the same.

I reach a hand for my swollen eye instinctively, and try to angle myself in the shadows.

"Hey, Darce. Mind if I ask you a few questions?" He smiles, opening his hands in an easy-going gesture. "All routine, I assure you."

"Uh, okay." I glance at Clay standing behind him, his eyes shooting daggers my way. I wave a hand towards one of the chairs. "Please, have a seat. What do you need to know?"

Topher nods and lowers himself into the chair closest to me. He pulls out a notebook and pen. "You can start by telling me what happened there." He points towards my face.

Out the corner of my eye, I can see Clay's lips press into a thin line. "Oh, this? It was nothing." I lower my chin. "I'm so clumsy sometimes."

"You're saying you did this to yourself?"

"Not on purpose, of course. But yes. Tripped over my own feet. Right there on the corner of the rug." I point to the frayed edge that's seen better days. "I caught my face on the arm of the chair." Behind him, Clay nods his approval.

"I see." Topher follows my gaze. "If you don't mind, Mr. Ferriman, I'd like to speak to Darcy alone."

"Why? You can see she's fine. She said so herself."

"Did she?" He stands, clasping his hands. "Is there something you don't want her to tell me?"

Clay scoffs. "No."

"Then you won't mind giving us a moment, will you?"

Clay swipes a hand across his mouth then rubs it down his jaw. "Darcy?"

"It's okay, Clay." He meets my gaze, and I give a slight nod. The children have been through enough today, I'm not going to have them watch their father be led away by the police.

"Fine," he seethes, walking down the hall to our bedroom, where I'm sure he'll be listening anyway.

Topher tucks his notebook into his pocket and leans forward in his seat. "Darcy, are you sure everything is okay here?"

Smoothing a hand down my thigh, I nod, keeping my eyes averted. "Mmhmm. Everything is fine."

He sighs, raking a hand through his hair and lowering his voice. "Camira and Holden are worried about you. If you need help, if—" he glances down the hall, "—if your husband did this—"

"He didn't," I interrupt, shaking my head. "He didn't do this." My voice warbles, but I remain steadfast. If Clay so much as thinks I'm saying anything against him, it'll only make things worse. Forcing myself to my feet, I hold my arm out in the direction of the door. "Now, if you don't mind, I have to tend to my children."

He holds my gaze for a beat before nodding resignedly. "Okay. Well, I hope that heals up quickly for you." He offers his hand, and I take it, feeling the card between our palms. "If you change your mind," he says quietly, then strides for the door.

I wait until the car headlights have disappeared from view before I allow myself to breathe again, my body sagging against the back of the chair.

Clay ambles out of the bedroom, smoke wafting after him and a glazed expression in his eyes. "That's my girl."

If he wants to believe I did this for him, he can go ahead, but I know the truth. I will never do another thing to benefit him. From now on, everything is for the children, and the children only.

CHAPTER TWENTY-THREE

HOLDEN

"You've gotta be kidding me," I grip the back of my neck, my eyes wide with rage. "You left her there?"

"I had no choice, Holden. She wouldn't say a word against him, said she did it to herself." Topher shrugs. "It's out of my hands unless she lays a complaint. I'm sorry."

"This is bullshit and you know it."

"It's the law, and it's my job to uphold it."

"Yeah? Well, isn't it also your job to protect the vulnerable?" I wave my hand out. "If she stays there, he'll end up killing her."

"You don't know that. Statistically speaking—"

"Don't go spouting your fucking statistics at me. You and I both know these things never end well. Hell, look at what happened to Jeri. You can't tell me you don't remember when that went down." We'd been ten at the time, but news travels fast in a small town like Brookhaven, and everyone was talking about the man who beat his wife to death.

Topher presses his thumbs to his closed eyes. "I remember, I do. But it doesn't change the fact I can't do anything about it right now. If she won't press charges and refuses to acknowledge he's done anything, then there's nothing I can do."

"Fuck!" My fist connects with the wall, leaving a dent.

"Woah." Cami jumps back. "I'm angry too, but we can't go destroying the place. Think how that will look if she *does* end up coming here for help."

As much as I don't want to admit it, she has a point. Taking my frustrations out on the walls and furniture is only going to make things worse. I want Darcy to feel safe with me, not like she's walked from one abusive man to another.

Dropping down on the couch, I rest my head in my hands. "I'll fix it tomorrow."

"Thanks for going out there, Topher. I appreciate your help," Cami says. "But I'll take it from here." She ushers him towards the door, pushing it closed behind him with a soft click.

The couch dips as she sits next to me, and a glass of whiskey hovers beneath my nose. "Here. I think we could both do with a drink."

I take it, slugging it back in one go. It burns on the way down.

"I don't know what to do," I admit, my voice hoarse.

She leans back, her glass cradled in her lap. "I don't either."

"When I saw her hunched over in the car…"

Her hand finds mine. "I know."

"Why does she stay?" I slump back against the cushions. "Why would she cover for him?"

"Maybe she feels like she has no other choice?" She shrugs. "That first day I went out there, she told me 'she'd made her bed', like she'd just accepted that it was her lot in life."

"Jesus." All I want to do is run out there, throw her over the back seat of my bike, and take her somewhere he can never find her, but I know that's not the answer. "I swore to myself I'd protect her after James died. If he were here, this never would've happened."

"No, a lot of things would be different if he were still around, but he's not. And aside from a mother still grieving, we're all she's got."

I launch up, almost knocking Cami's glass from her hand in the process. "What about Diane?"

"What about her?"

"Surely if anyone can get through to her, it's her mother."

Cami winces. "I don't know. You haven't seen her lately. She's… different now. In a world of her own most of the time."

"You don't think she'd want her daughter and grandkids safe though?"

She sits forward. "Bro, you noticed her bruises and how withdrawn she was the instant you saw her, and I know for a fact Diane has been out there to visit those kids. She told me herself. It's the only way I knew she'd had Bobby." She shakes her head. "You can't tell me she doesn't know what's going on."

I can't even begin to comprehend what she's saying. It's bordering on insane. Diane was the most caring, considerate woman when we were growing up. She always had a plate of cookies and a kind word. Sure, things went downhill when James passed away suddenly, but wouldn't that be even more reason to protect the ones you love? If she knew, she would've done something. I'm sure of it.

"What other options do we have?"

She huffs out an exasperated sigh. "None."

"It's settled then." I grab the keys. "Come on. We're going to pay Diane a little visit."

CHAPTER TWENTY-FOUR

HOLDEN

I don't need this shit right now. I've spent the past few days trying to talk some sense into Diane, and so far, I've gotten nowhere. She refuses to believe Darcy wouldn't tell her if Clay was abusive. I'm beginning to think it was a waste of time.

And now, on top of all that, I have to face the fucker and somehow manage not to punch his face to a bloody pulp. Seeing Clay is the last thing I want to be doing, but Jericho insists I be here because I was at the warehouse with him. He and Hannibal came to some sort of arrangement regarding the arsenal of weapons in storage, both ornamental and other, but the drugs are something he can't and won't ignore. Thankfully, we're all in agreeance on that.

Hannibal stands at the head of the table, in Jericho's usual spot. His stance is wide, his hands clasped in front of him. If I didn't already know he used to be Dante's right-hand man, I would've easily picked it from the way he carries himself. The guy is built like a tank, and I have no doubts he knows how to swing a punch or two.

Raised voices outside signal the arrival of Clay. Both Dustin and Stubbs have been given the task of bringing him in after a pat down.

The door swings open, and Clay is shoved forward, his arms held behind his back by Dustin. Stubbs walks over to one of the seats, pulls it out, and Clay is forced into it. They each take up position beside him in case he makes a run for it.

"What the fuck is going on?" Clay demands. "You can't go removing a guy from work with no explanation." His eyes roam the room, landing on me, and he snarls. "What the fuck are *you* doing here?"

I fight the urge to get up in his face, instead choosing to fold my arms across my chest. "This is my club, my work. I'm right where I should be."

"I apologise for the inconvenience. This won't take long." Hannibal steps up to the table, his fingers pressing into the edge as he leans forward. "I understand Mr. Takanawa has hired you to deliver goods to my warehouse."

Clay sniffs, his head swivelling to face Hannibal. "Your warehouse?"

Hannibal nods. "Mine."

He shifts in his seat. "Oh, ah, then yeah. What of it?"

"What exactly are these goods you're delivering for him?"

He shrugs. "I'm just the delivery guy."

"Cut the crap," Jericho says, his eyes narrowed. "You know exactly what you're delivering."

He leans back in his seat, bringing his hands to rest on the table. "Alright, so I know what I'm delivering. I didn't know it was common knowledge." He turns to Hannibal again. "Cases of ammo."

Hannibal nods, walking around the table so he's directly in front of Clay. "*Just* cases of ammo?"

He lifts a shoulder. "That's what I said, isn't it? What is all this?"

"You see, I have it on good authority that you're using my warehouse to store your own goods. Goods that I'm not interested in being a part of."

Clay shifts in his seat. "I don't know what you're talking about. I just pick up the boxes and deliver 'em." He splays his hands. "That's it."

"So you didn't meet with two drug dealers over the weekend then?" Hannibal leans on the table, giving him a pointed stare. "Think very carefully before you answer."

Stubbs and Dustin both place a hand on his shoulders, holding him down.

Sweat beads on his brow, and his voice shakes when he answers. "Why would I meet drug dealers? I don't even know any."

Hannibal thumps a fist on the table. "You think I'm an idiot?"

Clay shakes his head. "No."

"You're high as a fucking kite right now, and you have the audacity to lie to my face about it?"

He shifts in his seat again. "No… I… No." He glances to me as if I can save him. As if I'm not first in line to fuck him up. "You know me. I don't do that shit."

"Your eyes tell a different story, bro."

He rears back, like he's surprised I didn't jump to his aid.

"I saw you. I was there, at the warehouse. You sampled the goods and offered it to them too."

He shakes his head profusely, pointing a finger at me. "He's lying!"

"He's not." Jericho juts his chin. "We both saw you."

Hannibal raises a brow in Clay's direction. "You calling my colleagues liars?"

"I…I…"

"You might not know this, but the Hellhounds don't take too kindly to drug users and dealers in our town. In fact, we've made it a mission of sorts, to rid Brookhaven of scum like you." Jericho gives Stubbs a nod, and he squeezes Clay's shoulder a little harder, making him wince.

"B-but they're not local," he blurts out in a bid to save himself. "They don't deal from here." He huffs out an uneasy laugh. "Don't shit where you eat and all that."

"You think that makes it better?"

He frowns. "Yes? You said…" His eyes dart between Hannibal, Jericho, and me. "You said you don't want it here, in Brookhaven."

"Or in my warehouse," Hannibal adds. "Because I stand with the Hellhounds on this."

Clay nods. "Understood. I'll find somewhere else. Somewhere out of town?" He looks at Jericho for approval, but he doesn't get it.

"Oh that's cute," Dustin says, slapping his hand against Clay's shoulder. "He thinks it's that easy."

"I've taken over the Costello business, and that brings with it certain expectations. I can't be seen to be lenient on people who try to take me for a ride." Hannibal steeples his fingers, bringing them to his lips.

"But I wasn't... I didn't mean to..." Once again, he turns to me. "I just wanted to make her see I can provide."

I lunge across the table, taking his throat in my hand. "Don't you bring her into this." Fingers grapple with my hand, pulling me off him, and Jericho drags me back to his side, a steadying hand placed on my shoulder. "It has nothing to do with Darcy, and everything to do with your selfish needs and addiction." Raking a hand through my hair, I grip the back of my neck. "She deserves so much better than you."

"Gentlemen, please." Hannibal raises his hands. "Let's get back to the matter at hand, shall we?" He gives Dustin a nod, and he takes hold of Clay's hand, pushing it flat against the table.

"Which one?" Hannibal asks, retrieving a small blade from his pocket and wiping it with a cloth.

Clay's face drains of colour, and he gasps. "What?"

"Which. One?"

Beside me, Jericho tenses, but he won't undermine Hannibal in front of Clay. When we'd told him what we knew, he'd said he would handle it his way, and Jericho agreed. It's not the way of the Hellhounds, but it's not our call.

"I don't…"

Hannibal stabs the blade between two of his fingers, and Clay flinches. "Either you choose, or I do."

"I don't…"

"Eenie, meenie, minie…"

"This one!" He wiggles his pinkie. "Take that one." His voice cracks, and he closes his eyes, turning his head away so he doesn't have to see.

Hannibal raises the blade in the air and plunges it down hard into Clay's flesh. He cries out, wrenching his hand backwards and cradling it to his chest.

Using the same cloth as before, Hannibal runs it down the length of the blade, wiping it free of blood. "Pleasure doing business with you. I hope we don't meet again."

CHAPTER TWENTY-FIVE

DARCY

The days have gone by in a blur. Blue and purple bruises have formed around my eye and cheekbone, and it's still a little swollen. My wire-rimmed glasses do little to hide it, and Clay won't let me leave the house until it's cleared up. The children have had to miss out on preschool the rest of the week. I've poured all my focus into keeping them entertained with games and stories, movies and building forts. My daily chores have slackened, and so far, Clay hasn't said a word about it. He's swayed between ignoring me and barking out the odd few words, and the rest of the time he's busied himself in his garage. I don't know what he's doing in there, and I don't care. He could have a whole other family in there, and it wouldn't bother me. As long as he leaves me and the children alone, we're good.

I haven't seen or heard from Cami or Holden since the fair. I know it was them who sent Sergeant Grayson out, and while I appreciate the sentiment, it's too little too late. I'm sure they're upset with me for not saying anything, and I don't blame them. I'd be angry too if I tried to help someone who threw it back in their face. But Clay has made it abundantly clear there's no escaping him, so I give up. He's obviously realised that too, because he went back to work yesterday. No more babysitting for me.

Content to be the perfect mother to my children, and a half-hearted homemaker, I've accepted my life for what it is.

Lying on the floor, staring up at the fort blankets billowing in the breeze coming through the window, I listen to Molly chatter about how this is a castle and she's the princess. Bobby is setting his bath boats up around the perimeter to form the moat. Clay will be home for lunch soon, and I know he's going to hate that we've taken over the lounge floor, but I'm beyond caring. If he wants to sit and smoke, he can do so outside.

Tyres slowly crunch up the drive, and I ease myself out from the fort. I suppose I should fix him something to detract from the mess. Better he be fed than take it out on the kids.

Rummaging in the fridge, I pull out some salami and cheese, thumping them on the counter. There's a light tap on the door and a "Yoohoo," then my mum appears around the corner, her arms laden with bags of food.

Molly and Bobby both cry out in unison, "Grandma!" They race up to her, flinging their arms around her and nearly knocking her off balance. She doesn't scold them, simply laughs it off.

"You two, let Grandma get through the door before smothering her please." They groan and let her go, traipsing back to their fort, and throwing me the stink eye. I stifle my laughter behind my hand, then remember myself and quickly duck my head forward, combing my fingers through my hair to pull it over my eye. But it's too late. By the look on her face, she's already seen.

Her eyes go wide, and she almost drops the bags before quickly settling them on the counter. She moves to me with her arms outstretched and tears in her eyes. "Oh, baby," she whispers. "What has he done to you?"

Unbidden, my own eyes fill with tears, and I try to blink them away, to no avail. "Mum," I squeak, rushing into her arms. She crushes me to her chest, her hand stroking circles on my back as we sob together.

When we finally pull apart, she brushes my hair from my face and inspects the bruising. "They told me he was hurting you, but I didn't believe them." Her lips form a tight line. "I should've seen the signs. I should've paid more attention."

"It's not your fault."

"It's not yours either. I hope you know that."

Shaking my head, I stare down at my feet. She takes my hand and leads me to the table, pushing me into one of the chairs.

"How long has this been going on? Why have you never said anything?"

"I didn't know how." My voice is broken and raw. "You were always so sad after Dad… I didn't want to make it worse."

"Oh, my darling. I know I haven't been the mother I should've been, but you have to know I would've dropped everything if I thought…" Her voice trails off as she traces a finger along my bruised cheekbone. "I'm so sorry I wasn't there for you."

I smile through my tears. "You were."

"You don't have to lie to me." She pats my hand. "When Cami and Holden came out to see me, I didn't want to hear what they had to say, but they're so stubborn." She chuckles. "They kept coming over, talking to me, telling me how much you need me." She pulls her lips in between her teeth, sucking in a breath. "I've missed out on so much these past few years—" her voice falters, "—too caught up in my own grief to see how much you were hurting too." Her hands enclose mine. "You can't stay here with him."

"I don't have much choice. I tried to leave, and this is what I got." I remove my glasses and gesture to my face. "I've never seen him like that before, and I'm scared what he'll do if I ever try again." I glance to the children still playing in the fort. "I'd never forgive myself if he took it out on them instead."

"Then you understand how *I* can't leave you here with him either."

"What am I supposed to do, Mum? This is how I protect them. By staying."

"And who's going to protect you? Hmm?" Her brows rise. "There's only so much a body and mind can take. If I leave you here…" She closes her eyes. "I can't lose you too," she whispers.

"You won't."

She squeezes my hand, ducking her chin to meet my gaze. "If you stay here, I will." She says it as if it's a fact, and I suppose it is. The rage he showed on Tuesday as his fists rained down on me was nothing short of terrifying. He's never been like that with me before.

"I need time to think."

She tuts, her brow furrowing. "I don't see what there is to think about."

"Please, Mum. My head's all over the show right now. Give me a day or two to think, okay?"

"I don't like the thought of you being here with him. All this way out of town…"

I place my hand on hers. "I'll be fine."

She makes a strangled sound in the back of her throat.

"I promise." I check the clock on the wall and let out a sigh. "But right now, you can't be here. He'll be home soon, and if he sees you… It won't be good."

She swallows audibly then nods. "Okay. But I'm not giving up on you, and neither are those friends of yours." She drags me into her arms again and kisses my cheek. "You mean a lot to them, you know." She calls out a goodbye to the children. "Look after your mum for me, okay?" she says, giving them each a kiss on the top of their heads. "And don't tell Dad I was here, okay?" She whispers that last part, drawing her finger across her lips like a zipper.

Bobby nods, mimicking her action, and after watching her brother do it, Molly does the same.

She gives them a high five, then a wave and them casts a worried glance my way before leaving. I watch out the window as she navigates the drive, then pack away the food she brought before Clay comes home and sees it.

"Mummy?" Bobby stands behind me, his hands rolled into fists and tucked into his armpits. "Are we going to live with Grandma?"

I let out a sigh. I didn't realise he'd been listening in on our conversation. "No, sweetheart. I don't think that's a good idea."

He frowns, but his head bobs up and down in a slow nod. Not the reaction I expected.

"Why? Would you want to do that? Go and live with Grandma?"

He shrugs. "I don't know. Maybe." He takes a deep breath. "Why is Daddy always so angry?"

Dropping to my knees, I pull him into my arms. "I don't know, baby."

"Is it me and Molly? Did we do something?" he asks, and when I pull back, his eyes are wide and brimmed with tears.

"Oh, honey, no. You haven't done a single thing wrong."

"But we told him about your friends."

Brushing a hand across his jaw, I settle it on his shoulder. "Having friends isn't a reason to be angry." It's as I say the words that I realise the truth of them. "Daddy doesn't like to share me with other people."

"You tell us to share our things."

"I do. That's because sharing is a nice thing to do."

He scrunches his nose, deep in thought for a moment. "You can share my friends if you want."

And that right there? That's what changes my mind. My four-year-old has a better grasp on how to be a decent human being than my husband, and I won't have him corrupted.

"Thank you, sweetheart. That's very kind of you."

He smiles, wrapping his chubby arms around my neck and pressing his cheek to mine. I inhale deeply, taking in that fresh, soapy smell that children have.

"Maybe it *would* be nice to go and stay with Grandma for a while. What do you think?"

CHAPTER TWENTY-SIX

HOLDEN

That wasn't how I expected my morning to go, but I have to admit, I took satisfaction in watching him squirm. The flesh wound was the icing on the cake. I didn't have to raise a finger, and he still got to feel a taste of what Darcy has had their whole marriage. Karma can be a bitch sometimes, and I like it.

After Hannibal left, Jericho had Zeb wrap his hand in bandages and drive him to the hospital with his pinkie in a plastic bag of ice. I doubt they'll be able to do anything. Serves him right. It can serve as a reminder of what happens when you fuck with the wrong people. That even though he likes to throw his fists around with those weaker than he is, there is always someone farther up the food chain who can give it back just as good.

I wish I could see the look on Darcy's face when she sees what's happened to him. To be a fly on the wall for that moment would be pure gold. Unfortunately, I have work to do.

Thanks to our little meeting, I'm running behind. I'll have to work late tonight to get through it all. Not that it matters. I'm not really in the mood to socialise after hours at the moment. My head is too full of Darcy and the way she looked slumped over in the front seat of her car. If Diane doesn't come through, I'm going to have to take matters into my own hands and try to convince her myself. I really don't want to be the arsehole guy who steps in and tries to control her, but it's looking like that's what it'll come down to. I can't stand the idea of her and those kids out there with him. Especially now I know he's using. That shit fucks with your head, and it certainly explains his erratic behaviour. Not that there's any excuse for what he's done to her.

Aside from the day I left, this has been the hardest week of my life, knowing she's hurting, and I can't do a damn thing to help.

Pulling on my overalls, I climb into the pit and call to Cassian to bring the car over. While I wait, I do my toolbox check and make sure I have what I need for the muffler replacement.

Tyres squeal across the smooth concrete floor as Cassian pulls the car around. He lines it up and drives over top until I yell out for him to stop. The engine is almost deafening from down here, and when he cuts it off, my ears ring.

He climbs out, sticking his head beneath the front wheel. "Need any help?"

"Nah, kid, I got this one. Can you bleed the brakes on Mrs. Harris's beamer though?"

He gives me a salute. "Sure thing."

Someone switches the radio on, and the thumping sound of AC/DC's *Dirty Deeds* blasts through the speakers. I snort out a laugh at the irony of it. What Clay's been up to, what we just witnessed Hannibal do, it's all a bunch of dirty deeds.

Locating the exhaust clamps, I give them a spray of WD40 and while I wait for it to soak in, I remove the sump bung and drain the oil. May as well knock out both jobs in one go.

Once I have the clamps off, I work the muffler away from the pipe and toss it aside. The new one fits on easily, and I apply a sealant before pushing the two ends together and tightening the clamps.

Cassian sticks his head beneath the car again. "Someone to see you."

"Be right there." I wipe my hands on the rag hanging from my back pocket and climb out of the pit. Diane is there, wringing her hands together. "Everything okay?"

"You were right."

I stop midstride. "You've seen her?" She nods. "How is she?"

"Oh, Holden, she looks awful. Her face…" She hovers her hand in front of her left eye. "She's all battered and bruised."

My fingers flex involuntarily, forming fists by my sides. "Is she going to leave?"

"I'm not sure. I think I got through to her, but she's a stubborn thing, like her father."

"Goddamn it!" I punctuate the last word with a thump on the side wall. Diane jumps, holding her hand to her chest. "Sorry." I force my hands to loosen. "I just want her out of there."

She takes a tentative step towards me and places her hand on my arm. "I do too. Now that you've opened my eyes to see what was staring me right in the face, I can't stomach the thought of her with him a moment longer." Her already red-rimmed eyes fill with tears. "I feel wretched that I didn't see it before."

"You can't blame yourself. We see what we want to see sometimes."

"Yes, but I'm her mother. I should've seen. If it wasn't for you and Cami… I don't know that I would've ever noticed. Not until it was too late." Her voice cracks, and she dabs at her nose with a tissue.

"We can't think like that, Diane." I take her hands in mine. "We'll find a way. I'll go see Topher again. Maybe there's another avenue we haven't tried."

Her palm meets my cheek. "You're such a good boy. I'm so glad you're here keeping an eye on her for me."

"I just wish I could do more."

CHAPTER TWENTY-SEVEN

DARCY

Clay didn't come home for lunch. He's never done that before. I don't know whether I should risk leaving right now while we have the chance, or whether it's a test and he's really parked down the road, ready to collect me on the run.

I suppose there's only one way to find out. Picking up the phone, I dial the number for Lyman's Seeds. It rings three times before the receptionist answers, her perky voice too cheery for even me. When I give her my name and ask for Clay, there's a muffled sound, like her hand is over the receiver, and then another gruff voice comes on the line.

"Mrs Ferriman?"

"Yes?"

"This is Eric Lyman, manager of the plant. I believe we met one Christmas a few years back."

"Oh yes, I remember. How are you?"

He hesitates. "A little confused, to be honest with you, Mrs Ferriman. Clay came into work this morning, only to be dragged out of here by two rather intimidating men. We haven't seen him since."

It's wrong to feel a spark of hope ignite in your chest when you find out your husband has been taken hostage, but that's what happens. A tiny spark worms its way through my veins, lighting me up from the inside.

"Oh. Do you know why, or where they took him?" I try for a concerned voice, but I'm not sure how convincing it is.

"No, I was hoping you might be able to shed some light on the situation."

"Sorry, no. He doesn't really talk to me about his work dealings. He left this morning, like normal, and hasn't come home for lunch. That's why I was calling. I thought he might be doing overtime."

"Yes, well, we haven't seen him either. If you could get him to contact us on his return, that would be much appreciated."

"Will do." I press the end button and lean my back against the wall, my hand hanging loose in front of me. It seems like fate is on our side today.

"Bobby, Molly, you know how I said we might go and visit Grandma? Well, we're going to go there now." I smile, pushing off from the wall and gathering them in my arms. "Quickly go and pack a bag."

My palms sweat the whole drive into town, and I have to keep wiping them on my pants, so they don't slip off the steering wheel. I never made it past the gate last time, and now, here I am driving down the main street of Brookhaven, all thoughts of Clay at the back of my mind.

"Look!" Bobby points out the window. "That's Grandma's car."

And it is. Parked on the road outside Lawson's Lugs. I pull in behind her and turn to the kids. "I'll be just a moment, okay? I'm going to run in and let her know we're coming to stay and grab a key. You're in charge, Bobby." I hold my pinkie out to him, and he wraps his own around it.

"You can count on me."

"I knew I could." Climbing out of the car, it all feels surreal. I'm here, in town, without Clay knowing what I'm doing. I'm here of my own free will, and it feels glorious. The fact that I'm standing outside Holden's workplace may have a little something to do with it too.

I walk down the alley to the carpark out back, shielding my eyes against the sun. Mum is standing with her back to me, talking to Holden. My mouth goes dry, and my legs start to wobble as if they're made of jelly, but I force them on.

His eyes find mine before I've made it over, and the look on his face takes my breath away. There's a fierceness in his stare, but it's softened by his boyish grin.

Mum turns around, and her hands go to her mouth. "Darcy!" she cries, running to me and wrapping me in her arms. "Does this mean what I think it means?"

I nod as fresh tears form in the corner of my eyes. "It does. I'm leaving him."

"What made you change your mind?"

"Honestly, it was something Bobby said. I promised myself I wouldn't do anything for Clay anymore, only the children, and I realised I wasn't doing them any favours by exposing them to his moods." I hold my hands aloft. "We were wondering if we could come and stay?"

Mum throws her hands in the air, laughing. "Of course you can!" She grips Holden's hand suddenly. "Thank you for this."

"Nothing to thank me for."

She shakes her head at him, then turns to me. "Where are those grandchildren of mine? I want to go and give them a squeeze."

"Out front. We're parked behind you."

"Fabulous. I'll leave you two to talk. I can take the kids with me, if you like?" She holds her hands in a prayer-like position.

"Oh no, that's not necessary. This is a big change for them; I should probably be there for it. I won't be long."

"Take as long as you need. I'll stay with them until you're done." She waves over her shoulder as she walks away.

"This is… Wow." Holden rakes a hand through his hair, grinning. "You're doing the right thing."

I nod, returning his smile. "I know. I feel… lighter. Like a weight has gone from my shoulders."

"I'm not surprised. It was a pretty heavy weight to be carrying by yourself all these years." He reaches out, tucking a strand of hair behind my ear, and I can't help but lean into his palm. His thumb circles my lips ever so softly. "If you ever need a break from your mum, I have space at mine. Me and Cami had it all set up for…" He stops, scrunching his nose. "Doesn't matter."

"You would do that for me?"

He leans in, pressing his forehead to mine. "I would do anything for you."

My breath hitches, my eyes falling closed as I tilt my chin. He closes the gap, his hand trailing down to cup my jaw as his lips press to mine. Softly at first, then with all the want and need of a lifetime. It's as if time ceased to exist, and all that's left is us and this kiss.

There's a whistle, then a slow clap from behind. "About bloody time." Matiu saunters up, cigarette hanging from his lips. "He's only been pining after you half his life."

Holden chuckles, swinging his arm around my shoulders. "He's not wrong."

I nestle into him, my palm pressed against his chest. This is what safe feels like.

CHAPTER TWENTY-EIGHT

HOLDEN

"I should call Cami and let her know what's going on." I pull my phone out and quickly dial her number.

She answers straight away. "What's up, loser?"

"Is that any way to speak to your favourite brother?"

"My *only* brother," she corrects.

"You know, I was going to share some good news with you, but now I don't think I will."

"That's okay, I'm good at guessing. Did you find a winning lotto ticket on the ground and we're now millionaires?"

"First off, if *I* found the winning ticket, that would make *me* the millionaire, not you. But no, that's not it."

"Rude. I'd share it with you if I won."

"No you wouldn't."

"I mean, I'd give you a couple bucks. Cover the rent from the past few weeks at least."

"How giving of you."

"I know, right? It's one of my best qualities." Her voice goes low and breathy, like a cheesy perfume commercial. "I'm just such a giver."

"Sure you are. Anyway, do you want to hear my news or not?"

"Depends. Does it benefit me at all?"

"It might."

"Oh my God. Is it Diane? Did we convince her to go see her?" There's a rustle down the line, followed by footsteps.

"We did, and it worked." I glance down at Darcy. "She's standing right here beside me." I hand her the phone.

"Hey, Cami."

There's a squeal, and Darcy has to pull the phone away from her ear with a laugh. I leave them to chat while I fill Matiu in on everything.

"Shiiit. I miss out on all the fun." He pouts. "This bloody wedding, man. It's taking up too much of my life."

Laughing, I slap a hand to his shoulder. "That's only the beginning, bro. Think what it'll be like once she starts spitting out babies."

"Oh Jesus. I'm fucked, aren't I?"

"Probably." I cast my gaze across to Darcy, laughing into the phone. "But I think I'm just as fucked as you."

There's a squeal of tyres as a car takes the entry too fast, and I bolt towards Darcy out of instinct. The truck screeches to a stop and Clay stumbles out, his hand bandaged and his eyes fiery as hell. "Where is she?" he demands, stomping towards Matiu.

He widens his stance, holding his palms up to stop him. "This is private property, man. You need to go."

"I'm not going anywhere without Darcy. I know she's here."

I step in front of her, one hand held to her hip, securing her to me. "There's nothing here for you, Clay. You need to leave."

He turns his attention on me and storms forward. "She's *my* wife!"

"That may be the case, but she doesn't want to be with you anymore. You scare her." I can feel her trembling, her hands clutching the fabric of my shirt.

"The fuck is going on out here?" Jericho marches over, eyeing Clay. "You've got some balls showing up here after this morning."

Clay points a shaking finger at me. "He's got my wife."

Jericho makes a point of looking at me then turns back to Clay. "Looks like she doesn't want to be your wife anymore."

"She can't just decide that," he spits.

"I hate to break it to you, but she can. That's how divorce works. And from the looks of her face, she's got every reason to leave." He steps up closer. "Now, I suggest you get back into your truck and go calm down somewhere else, or I'll have to call the cops."

Clay reaches around behind him and pulls out a gun, aiming it at Jericho. "I'm not going to say it again. Give me my wife."

Jericho holds his hands up. "You don't want to do this."

"The fuck I don't." He swings the gun to me then back to Jericho. "She's *mine*."

She slips from my grasp before I can stop her. "Okay, Clay," she whispers, her hands outstretched. "I'll come with you. Just don't hurt anyone."

"Darcy, no." I grab for her arm, but she shakes me off, her tear-filled eyes meeting mine. "I'm sorry," she says. "I have to go with him. I can't let him hurt anyone else."

"But he's going to hurt you! Darcy, please."

She shakes her head, walking over to him with slow steady steps. Once she's within reach, he pulls her back against his chest and holds the gun to her temple. Her lips form the words '*I love you*', then she closes her eyes. "You're going to let us walk out of here or I'll shoot her in the head. The kids too."

I fall to my knees, watching in horror as the woman I've loved my whole life is taken from me again. He backs down the alley, half lifting, half dragging Darcy with him until they're out of sight.

A loud boom resounds down the alley from the street, followed by screaming. Car doors slam, and tyres squeal.

"Fuck!" I climb to my feet and run down the alley to see Clay spin the wheel and the car speed off down the road. On the sidewalk is Diane, a pool of blood beneath her.

Footsteps come up behind me, and Matiu stops short. "Oh shit." He takes two steps towards Diane, then back to me, as if he doesn't know what to do.

"I have to follow them. Check on her." I race back up to the carpark, throw my leg over my bike and kick it into gear, slapping my helmet on.

"What are you doing? Are you crazy?" Jericho calls out. "You can't go after them."

"The fuck I can't. I've only ever loved one woman, and it's her. I have to do this." I peel out of the lot before he can stop me. I'll never forgive myself if anything happens to Darcy or those kids. They'll already be scarred having to watch their father shoot their grandmother in cold blood.

I race down the alley and out onto the road, following them down the main street and onto the long stretch of road towards their house. The car swerves across the centre lane, narrowly avoiding an oncoming van. I can see Bobby's head peering out the back window, his eyes wide with fear.

Fucking Clay Ferriman. Who the fuck does he think he is, scaring them like this?

They take the next turn sharply, careening across to the other side of the road then cutting back into their lane. Thank Christ there wasn't a car coming their way this time.

The sign announcing the lake district swooshes past in a blur, and Clay takes another sharp turn. The front tyre bumps up over the sidewalk before righting itself and speeding towards the shingle road of the new subdivision being built. A cloud of dust blows up behind him, making it difficult to see, but I catch a glint off the rooftop and follow on.

I pass orange road cones dotted along the way, and though I can't see too far, I can hear the rumble of machinery ahead, and I hope to God Clay has heard them too.

CHAPTER TWENTY-NINE

DARCY

"Clay, please. You're scaring the children." I brace my hands on the car door and dashboard. "You have to slow down."

"Don't tell me what to do!" he screams, pressing his foot to the floor. The car jerks forward, and behind me, Molly lets out a wail.

"It's okay, sweetheart," I coo, reaching a hand back to wrap around her knee. "Everything's going to be okay." I try to put as much conviction into my voice as I can, even though inside I'm screaming in terror. I never should've tempted fate by seeing Holden. It was so stupid of me to leave the car parked out on the road for him to see, and with the children inside, no less. If only I'd let Mum take them with her, they'd be safe, and she'd still be… A sob breaks loose, and I clutch a hand to my chest. The way her body just crumpled to the ground, her mouth wide in a silent scream. I'll never be able to shake that image from my mind. Though, after today, perhaps I won't live long enough to have to.

You can't think like that. Be strong. For the children.

Dust billows up around the car, and I can barely see two feet in front of us. I know they've been building apartments around here, and a restaurant to overlook the lake, but I can't quite tell which part we're in. Everything looks the same.

"Please, Clay," I try again. "It's me you're angry with. Let the children go. They've done nothing wrong."

He turns to me with hatred shining in his eyes. "*You* brought them into this, not me."

I can't believe him right now. It's always my fault. Nothing is ever good enough.

"Can't you see what you're doing to them? To me?" I gesture at my tear-stained face covered in bruises. "This isn't a marriage, Clay."

"What would you call it then? I provide for you, give you a roof over your head, clothes on your back. You and the children don't go without. Sounds like a marriage to me."

"What about love?" I whisper, sniffing and wiping my tears.

"This *is* love. Everything I do is for you. I love you so fucking much, and you won't love me back." He turns tormented eyes on me. "And if I can't have your love, then neither can he." The car careens across the road then swerves back again.

"Clay, please!" I point out the windscreen. "Watch the road!"

He sniffs, then slowly turns back in time to see a line of flashing lights pop up in front of us. "Shit!" He wrenches the steering wheel to the left, and the tyres lock, the car spinning out. Molly screams.

The car lurches up and over something, and for a brief moment, I feel weightless, like a bird in flight. Then just as suddenly, there's a loud crunch, and everything goes black.

Chapter Thirty

Holden

"No, no, no, no, no!" I pull the bike up to the bank of the lake in time to see the car hit the rise then plunge headfirst into its depths. Tossing my helmet aside, I yell out to anyone who can hear me to call an ambulance, then I dive in after them.

The bonnet is completely submerged, and both Clay and Darcy have their heads rested against the airbags that must've deployed on impact. Neither one is moving.

In the back, Molly is crying and kicking her legs, while Bobby stares out at me with wide eyes.

"Bobby!" I tap the glass, and he blinks slowly. "Bobby, I need you to listen to me, okay? I'm going to get you out of there, but I need your help. Can you do that? Can you help me?"

He blinks again, clearly in shock. His eyes dart back and forth.

"Bobby? I need you to do something for me, okay?"

He scrunches back into his seat, pulling his knees into his chest as water begins to flow in through the bottom of the door.

"Bobby!" I pound the flat of my hand on the window, and this time he sees me.

"Holden?" He presses his hand to the window, then slides it down to the handle, but it's no use. The water pressure is too much, and if I know Darcy, she'll have child locks on the doors anyway. There's no way these things are getting open.

"Bobby, I need you to undo your seatbelt and pull out the headrest." I point to the back of Darcy's seat, where she's still slumped over the dash.

He falls forward as his belt comes undone, then he grabs the headrest and pulls, but it doesn't move. I point at the button on the side.

"You need to push that."

He nods and does as I say.

"You're doing great, Bobby." I close my eyes. I've never had to break a car window before, but I imagine it takes some force. God, I hope this works.

I point at the metal stems at the bottom of the headrest. "I want you to try and hit the window as hard as you can with that, okay?" I mime hitting the glass to show him.

He stares down at the headrest then back at the window and begins to cry. "I don't think I can."

"You've got this, Bobby. Give it a try." I hold my breath as he rears back and rushes it toward the window. It does nothing. He tries again.

Nothing.

He swipes his sleeve across his tears and rears back once more, but the glass won't break.

"Okay, okay, you can stop." I hold my hand up, my eyes searching for anything that might help. When they land on the window rim, an idea surfaces.

"Here's what I want you to do. Get the pointy end and jam it as hard as you can into this." I point at the rubber rim. "As hard as you can, and hold it there. I'm going to try and push it in from out here."

He nods, lining the sharp end up and putting all his weight on it. There's a pop, and then movement in the glass. I spread my hands flat on the pane and wiggle it down until there's a crack at the top, and then I push with my shoulder. The window falls into the car, along with another gush of water.

Molly tips her head back and screams, her legs and arms flailing.

"It's okay, Molly. I'm going to get you out," I soothe, reaching in to undo her seat buckle. It's one of those four-pronged ones with the red button in the centre, and I can't seem to get it to work.

Bobby reaches down between my hands and yanks on something. The straps come loose and I'm able to wiggle Molly free. I pull her through the window and onto my hip then reach in for Bobby.

He glances to the front. "What about Mummy?"

"I'll come back for her, I promise. But I have to get you two out first." With my arms under his armpits, I drag him out too and wade towards the shore. There are people milling about, some on phones, I hope calling the paramedics. Some are filming.

One man in a high vis vest runs out into the water, taking the kids from me. "I've got them," he says. "I'll keep them safe." I give a nod and turn back to see the rest of the car has gone under.

CHAPTER THIRTY-ONE

DARCY

The sun beats down on my face as I tip it back and point at the clouds above. "That one looks like a cat," I say, and beside me, Molly giggles.

"No, it doesn't. It's a horse!"

"I can see a bird," Bobby adds, and his small hand moves in front of my face. "There's the beak, the wings, and the tail. See?"

I angle my head, squinting my eyes. "I guess it does sort of look like a bird."

"Look at the way that one curls around the others. Isn't it—" I suck in a sharp breath as something pounds against my chest.

"Mummy?" Molly whimpers, and I scramble for her hand, holding it tight. I can't seem to form words, just a raspy inhale, and with it comes another sharp pain.

I try to draw breath again, but I can't. The air has gone, vanished, and in its place is a cloying sense of heaviness. It's too thick to breathe.

I sputter, my body convulsing, and then all of a sudden, my ears are filled with noise. People yelling, someone crying, and an incessant beeping sound in the distance.

"Darce?" I blink against the harsh light to see Holden's face hovering over me. His hair is wet and stuck to his face, and he's breathing funny. Perhaps he can feel it too, that heaviness.

"Mummy?" Molly throws herself across me, her pudgy hands squeezing tight.

"Here, let's help you up." Holden lifts Molly and plonks her down beside him, then wraps his arm behind my shoulders and hoists me upright. My body feels heavy and exhausted, like I've run a marathon, and I collapse into his chest. He wraps one arm around me and one around Molly.

"What… happened?" I reach up to touch my head and feel wetness. Was I in the shower? Did I fall?

Holden's voice vibrates through my chest as he tells me, "You had an accident."

My eyebrows pinch together, and I shake my head. I would remember something like that, wouldn't I?

"Your car went into the lake."

"It did?" My eyes widen then blink closed against the bright sunlight. A flash of Clay driving erratically dances in my mind. The sound as we hit the bank, and the crunch of the bumper hitting the water. My hand flies to my mouth. "Oh my God."

"You're okay. The children too." There's an empty silence after, and I know without him telling me that Clay didn't make it. The tightness in my chest is back, and I rub at the spot, trying to ease the pain. There's no easing that ache though. The ache of losing someone you once loved, no matter how volatile. A sob falls from my lips, and Holden wraps his arm tighter around me, kissing the top of my head.

"Shh, you're okay."

Bobby crawls to my side, taking my hand in his. He leans his head against me. Molly pulls out of Holden's grasp and slides over to her brother, linking her arm through his.

"You know, it was Bobby who saved your life." Holden reaches down and ruffles his hair. "He was a real champion."

"No, I didn't. You did."

"Are you kidding? Without you helping me, I never could've got in and got you out."

I tilt my head up to look at Holden, my hand finding his cheek. "You pulled us out?"

He gives me an odd look, like it's obvious. "Of course I did."

"Why would you do that? Risk your life for us?"

Placing his hand over mine, he pulls it to his lips. "I told you I'd do anything for you."

"But risking your life? Cami would never forgive me if you died trying to save me."

"Pretty sure she'd kill me if I *didn't* try." I chuckle, kissing the tip of her nose. "And I'd never be able to live with myself if I let anything happen to you. In case you haven't noticed by now, I've been in love with you since the day we met."

"You have?"

He rolls his eyes. "Why do you think I left the day you got married?"

"*That's* why you left?"

"I couldn't bear to see you with someone else."

"I had no idea."

He huffs out a laugh. "Yeah. I kept it pretty close to my chest. Even Cami didn't know."

It's all so much to take in. In a matter of minutes, hours perhaps, I've not only discovered my husband of five years is dead, but the boy I fell in love with all those years ago, loves me back.

The distant sound of sirens carries on the air, and the crowd around us parts, making a path. Swirling lights grow closer, until the ambulance slows and comes to a stop on the road. Two paramedics rush over to us. One wraps blankets around the children and checks them over, while the other tends to me and Holden. To be safe, they want to take us all to the hospital for a full exam.

I grasp hold of Holden's hand as we're led to the ambulance. "You'll stay with me?"

His hand curls into my hair, gripping the base of my neck. "Of course. I'll stay as long as you'll have me."

CHAPTER THIRTY-TWO

HOLDEN

I never imagined it could feel like this. Having the woman of my dreams curled into my side while her children sleep in the other room is something I never dared to hope for. It's been a rough few weeks, and we still have a long way to go, but the children sleep a little more soundly now. Their trauma over nearly drowning, the shooting of their grandmother, and losing their father all in one go really messed with their heads, but we're taking each day as it comes.

It was an easy decision for them to move in here when we left the hospital. Plagued with nightmares, Darcy didn't feel safe anywhere else but by my side, and we had everything set up already, so it was a no-brainer. Of course, having Cami here to help wrangle the kids and play the cool aunty role she so desperately craved has been a Godsend too.

I'd be lying if I said I didn't have my own selfish reasons for wanting them here. After so many years yearning for something I never thought possible, I'm finally getting my shot. Waking up to her every morning is the highlight of my day, along with going to sleep at night with her curled into my side. Hell, even the in-between times are pretty fucking good.

She rolls over, threading her leg with mine. A small sigh slips from her lips, and she nestles into me. I bring both arms around her, pressing a kiss to her forehead, and she lazily tilts her chin upwards. Without her glasses on, the blue of her eyes stands out against the red halo of hair surrounding her, and she looks angelic. Far too angelic for the thoughts running through my mind of what I want to do to her right now.

"Good morning." She grins up at me, one finger tracing circles across my chest.

"Every morning with you is a good one." Jesus, when did I get so cheesy?

She giggles, burying her face in the crook of my shoulder. "I can't believe you just said that."

"Neither can I." I chuckle, pulling her tight against me. I only mean for it to be a hug, but she slides her body on top of mine, her hands resting on my chest.

"Is this okay?" she asks, her lip pulled between her teeth. God, she's beautiful.

I shift my hips beneath her, and her eyes widen. "Does it feel like it's okay to you?"

She nods, and I slide my hands to her waist. I don't want to rush things with her. I know the things he did to her, and I don't ever want her to feel trapped with me.

She presses her lips to my chest, then the base of my throat. I try to hold it in, but my body betrays me and I groan, low in my throat. Her eyes find mine, and she licks her lips, wiggling until her face hovers above mine. Slowly, our mouths meet, and my hands slide around to cup her arse.

She opens her mouth, moaning into mine, and it takes everything I have not to throw her on the bed and take her here and now.

Her legs slide down so she's straddling my hips, her soft heat pressed against my hard length. She brings her hands to my face, cupping my cheeks as she kisses me deeper. Her hips move in a tantalisingly slow circle, and I grip her arse, guiding her.

She breaks free of the kiss, pushing herself up to a sitting position. Her hand toys with the hem of her top, her lip pulled between her teeth again.

I stay her hand. "It's okay. We can wait."

She shakes her head. "No. I want this. Just…" She ducks her head, and with my finger curled beneath her chin, I tilt her face until I can see her eyes.

"What is it?"

"There are… scars."

"Okay."

"They're not pretty."

"There's nothing about you that isn't pretty. But if you don't want me to look, I won't." And I mean it.

"You can look," she whispers, peeling the loose tee over her head and tossing it aside. "I want you to see all of me." There are small, raised circles the size of a cigarette along her ribcage, and fading bruises along her collarbone. Jagged lines lace up her torso. I trail my finger over each one, and she closes her eyes, tipping her head backwards.

I pull my hand away. "Do you want me to stop?"

Her head makes the slightest movement. "No."

Cradling my hands behind her back, I sit so she's in my lap. My lips kiss her scars one by one, over her shoulder and collarbone, and anywhere I can see he's hurt her. It won't take away what he did, but perhaps it can take away some of the pain inside.

I kiss along her throat until she grabs hold of me and kisses me back with force. Her hips find a rhythm, and she rocks, sliding herself over me.

"I want you," she whispers against my lips. Who am I to tell her no?

Gripping her hips, I lift her until the tip of my cock pushes against her slick heat. Watching her eyes, I lower her gently down, inch by excruciating inch. She's so fucking warm and soft, and I hiss out a breath, lowering my forehead to her shoulder.

"So fucking good."

"Mmhmm," she murmurs, her hips already rolling. She clings to my neck, arching her back, and I lower my lips to one nipple, slowly laving my tongue around the tightened bud.

"Oh God." She leans back farther, her hips bucking faster and faster.

I tug her nipple between my teeth, just hard enough to get her attention, but not so hard it'll bring back memories. She cries out, and I clamp my hand over her mouth with a chuckle. "Shhh, we'll wake them, and I'm not finished with you yet."

My hand slides down her throat to her breasts, then on past her stomach. I find her clit, circling my thumb across it as she rocks into my hand.

"Oh shit, oh shit," she pants, her nails digging into my skin.

"That's it, Darce. Come for me, baby," I coax, flicking my thumb faster until all at once, her thighs tense, and she shudders, a breathy cry on her lips.

Grabbing hold of her hips, I rock them into me until her body relaxes and she collapses against my chest.

With my arms firm around her, I lay back on the mattress, bringing her with me. She nuzzles into me, letting out a contented sigh. I thread my fingers through her hair, brushing it off her shoulder and exposing her creamy skin.

"I don't know about you, but that's the best wake-up I've ever had."

Her shoulders shake as she chuckles. "It was definitely up there."

"Mummy!" The door handle rattles, followed by a tiny fist pounding on the wood. "Are you awake?"

Darcy's head snaps up, her eyes wide. "Do you think she heard me?" Her hand covers her mouth, but it doesn't hide her grin.

"Oh yeah, she *definitely* did." I grin, swatting her arse. "Come on, we'd better go out there before she breaks the door down."

"Hey, lovebirds!" Cami's voice carries over the thumping. "A little warning next time please. I had my ears open and everything." She cackles. "Oh, and your mum is here too, Darce."

Diane had been lucky. The hospital said the bullet missed all the vital organs, which saved her. After surgery and a lot of bedrest, she's slowly recovering. Apparently enough to make house calls now.

The look on Darcy's face is adorable. She's beet red, with wide eyes, and her mouth opening and closing like a goldfish.

I chuckle, wrapping her in my arms. "Don't look so worried."

"That's easy for you to say, it's not your mother out there hearing… what we just did." She hissed the last part, which only makes me laugh more.

"Darce, you have two kids. I think she knows you have sex."

Her hand clamps over my mouth as she glances towards the door. "Shhhh. Knowing and hearing are two different things, and she's in recovery."

"Oh." I nod. "So you're worried about her regressing because she heard us? I mean, sure, I suppose that's a possibility, but, and I'm just throwing ideas out here, maybe she'd just be happy to hear you're… being looked after." I grin, pressing my lips to hers. "Now, get up, woman. The longer you wait, the harder it is."

"What is?"

"The walk of shame."

She slaps her hand on my chest playfully, then pushes herself up, giving me a magnificent view.

"I'm not ashamed," she says, folding her arms across her chest and pushing her breasts up.

Goddamn, she's beautiful.

I roll over, discarding the sheet. "Good. Neither am I."

A Note from the Author

Thank you so much for taking the time to read *Break Loose*. I was asked to take part in a charity anthology last year, and from that, I ended up writing *Cut Loose*, and I knew I wasn't finished there. Thus, the Hellhounds series was created!

Hopefully you enjoyed reading it as much as I enjoyed writing it. If you did, I would love it if you could leave a review. Reviews not only help our work to be seen, they also offer valuable feedback.

Once again, thank you for reading!

Stacey xxx

ACKNOWLEDGEMENTS

At the start of the year, I set myself some goals. I had no idea whether I'd be able to meet them, but I did it all the same. Break Loose is the final book I had planned (though I'm already thinking of a Christmas novella!), and it was a doozy to get finished.

I can't tell you how many times I changed what was going to happen. I just knew it needed more, and I have to say, I'm so pleased with the final product.

To keep me on track, I started doing writing sessions with Indi and Debs, which really helped get my wordcount up. I can't thank them enough for their help and inspiration.

I also learned that I need incentives to fully embrace a deadline, so I enlisted the help of the BrickStore, BrickCollector, and various other Lego stores. Every time I was in a slump, I'd buy a new kit and not allow myself to use it until I'd reached my goal. This worked wonders!

Now, those incentives wouldn't be possible without the support (both financially and emotionally) of my wonderful husband, Aaron. He has been my rock from the day I started on this journey.

To my amazing friend and editor, Trina. You've been there from the start, and without you, I never would've had the courage to pursue this dream of mine.

Nicole, you're always there with an ear when I need to vent, or with a joking meme to get me back on task. I love that we bonded over books all those years ago and it's still standing strong.

I also need to give an extra thanks to Indi for your help with my cover. Your input really helped bring it to life. Thanks!

And of course, to all the readers out there who have taken a chance on this author, I appreciate each and every one of you. Thank you so much for coming on this crazy ride with me.

About the Author

Stacey resides in Ashburton, New Zealand with her husband and three children. She is a qualified proofreader, author, wife, mother, and self-proclaimed culinary goddess. When she's not busy writing or editing books, she enjoys reading and procrastinating on TikTok.

She absolutely loves hearing from readers, so please feel free to reach out via email, Instagram, or join her reader group, Broadbent's Bookish Babes.

www.staceybroadbent.com

OTHER BOOKS BY STACEY BROADBENT

Short Stories and Poetry
Musings, Mournings, and Misadventures
Musings, Mayhem, and Mystery

Anthologies
Scars to your Beautiful
Witching Hour: Vices and Virtues
The White Ribbon Collection
Key to my Heart
A Touch of Inspiration
No Place Like Home
Serendipity
Lucky Star
Hellhounds